But right now as the music flowed through me, I believed it. I believed that love was a special kind of heartbreak that only the brave dared to experience.

And I was not brave.

As I neared the end of the piece I lifted my head, blinking back the tears that welled in my eyes.

I turned toward the window as I played the last notes.

Though my fingers kept moving, my brain froze.

There was a man standing at the window. Watching me.

A tall, dark, and handsome man wearing a long black cloak and a top hat.

I should have been afraid. Would have been afraid.

Except that he looked more like an apparition than a dangerous man. He looked like he'd walked out of the past.

As I ended the song and the strains of the music lingered in the air, I came to a conclusion.

Grandpa might not be the only one who needed to have a psychological evaluation.

Perhaps I also needed to be evaluated.

DESTINED IN THE TWILIGHT

ALSO BY KATHRYN KALEIGH

THE BECQUERELS

Twist of Fate

When the Stars Align

Once in a Blue Moon

Once Upon a Christmas

A Wish Upon a Star

Written in the Wind

Scripted in the Stars

Destined in the Twilight

Promised in the Mist

Trapped in the Melody

When Lightning Strikes

Storm of Time

Midnight Storm

When the Moon Falls

Stormborn Angel

Time Tempest

The Heart Remembers

A Moment in Time

Moonlight Shadows

Rescued in Time

DESTINED IN THE TWILIGHT

THE BECQUERELS

INTO THE MIST

KATHRYN KALEIGH

DESTINED IN THE TWILIGHT

PREVIEW: PROMISED IN THE MIST

Written by Kathryn Kaleigh

Published by KST Publishing, Inc., 2022

Cover by Skyhouse24Media

www.kathrynkaleigh.com

❀ Created with Vellum

To learn more about Kathryn Kaleigh, visit

www.kathrynkaleigh.com

Kathryn Kaleigh

1

MACKENZIE BECQUEREL

I sat on the sofa in my Grandpa Jonathan's parlor, his cat looking up at me with obvious curiosity.

The cat was solid white with bright blue eyes. A hairball with eyes.

When did Grandpa get a cat, anyway?

I didn't need this additional piece of evidence that I had not been to visit my Grandpa enough.

When my phone vibrated in my jacket pocket, I glanced at the round analog clock on the wall across the room.

I didn't have any appointments right now, but it could be a client. Or a student.

Grandpa had stepped out to the foyer to answer his phone and I could hear him talking to someone, but couldn't understand his words.

The cat meowed at me.

I gave in to what I knew was a common and irritating addiction and checked the message on my phone.

It was not a client. It was my sister, Victoria.

VICTORIA: *Did you make it there yet?*

ME: *Yes. Waiting for Grandpa to get off the phone.*

I tucked the phone back in my pocket. I'd promised Victoria that I'd let her know when I got here.

Unfortunately for her, I was not good at that sort of thing.

But Victoria had generalized anxiety disorder. She'd always had anxiety, but since my sister Sophia disappeared ten years ago, it had gotten worse.

And now, we had not heard from our brother in over a month.

That's why I was here.

I knew Cameron had been here. He'd sent me a text telling me that he was spending some time here with Grandpa and working on a project.

Unlike Victoria, I hadn't worried when I hadn't heard from him in a couple of weeks. Cameron was like me in that way. He didn't like to check in with others when he could take care of himself.

But after a few days of no response from Cameron by text with calls going straight to voicemail, I had eventually called Grandpa.

He'd talked in vague phrases, suggesting that Victoria and I come for a visit.

But I'd asked specifically about Cameron.

Grandpa said Cameron's car was here, but he wasn't.

Since Grandpa was getting up in age and had been through a lot of stress lately—with his wife dying a few years ago, then my sister vanishing from his home—I knew I had to check on him.

If he was getting dementia, he'd have to be moved into a facility.

Since all us—me, Cameron, and Victoria—had careers, we could not take care of him.

My private practice was going gangbusters.

I'd had to reschedule a day of clients just to come here for two days. I was going to be working extra hours for at least a week, maybe two, to catch up. Some people worked five days a week with weekends off. Not me. I worked six days a week. Taught a class in the evenings and used Sundays to catch up on progress notes and prepare lectures for the following week.

In between clients I answered student texts. While I graded online exams, I took texts and calls from clients.

To say I had a busy schedule was an understatement.

Victoria suggested I work on boundaries. But Victoria had never taught today's instant gratification students, nor had she worked with clients in a crisis.

I did not fault her for not understanding. Most people couldn't.

I blamed it all on the Internet. Most websites had some kind of instant chat capabilities. We, as a society, were trained to get immediate responses on most things.

So when a student sent a message of any sort, they expected a response right away.

Not their fault either and I didn't judge them for it.

I was the same way.

But no one in my family understood.

Hence the boundaries criticisms that came phrased all sorts of different ways.

I did what it took to be successful.

Even if that meant I spent twelve hours a day tethered to my electronic devices, turning them off for fifty minute intervals between clients.

The cat meowed at me again.

"What?" I asked. "Am I in your chair?"

I stood up and the cat immediately jumped into my chair where I had been sitting.

"I guess that's a yes."

This was going to be an interesting visit.

2

ANDREW LAURENT

May 1854

I raced across the fallow fields, the movement of the horse powerful beneath me.

I liked that and the feel of the wind in my face.

And admittedly, I liked speed.

My horse, Lightning Bug, had been with me for years. I was pretty sure he was used to my occasional needs to race across a field.

My sister, Isabella, had named him. I'd been planning to change it to something more masculine, but I just never got around to it. So Lightning Bug had stuck.

There were worse names as far as names went.

I pulled on the reins, letting the horse know that we could stop now.

We walked slowly down the dirt road leading up to the front of my uncle's house, known as the Becquerel Estate.

I'd grown up in New Orleans, but my family had packed up

and moved here last year after a mishap with our property down there. The estate house had burned and the city house had to be sold to pay off remaining debt. There was enough money left for a new start.

My father was in the process of building his own house on some of mother's property adjacent to my uncle's.

In the meantime, we all lived in the big three-story house with my cousins.

Even though the house was plenty big for all us—two big families—I preferred spending time at the garçonnière, my cousin's bachelor's apartment. But lately he had begun wanting more privacy, so I was currently living here in one of the many guest rooms in the big old house.

As I rode beneath the large oak trees draping over the road, I thought maybe I'd go into town tonight.

Have a whiskey. Maybe go over to Natchez Under the Hill. It was a rather dangerous place, all in all, but I liked it. I actually liked the little thrill of danger that went with going someplace my father would have my head for going.

It wasn't that I was rebellious. It was just that I was used to living in New Orleans. Living here in the northern part of Mississippi after growing up in New Orleans, was a big adjustment and I didn't know if I would ever be ready to live the boring life of a cotton planter.

Instead, I worked hard during the day and played hard in the evenings.

Reaching the front of the house, I slid off the horse, looped the reins over the hitching post, and ran up the steps.

My cousin, Emma, met me at the door.

"There you are," she said. "I've been looking for you."

Emma was rather annoying as far as cousins went. And adding to her general annoyingness, her favorite pastime was playing the piano.

She played it all the time, especially delighting in playing for guests in the evenings.

She was a good enough player. But sometimes sitting there listening to her playing the piano for hour after hour was worse than watching paint dry.

"Mother is having some guests over tonight and she wants you to be here," Emma said with obvious excitement.

My spirits crumbled. If my Aunt Eloise wanted me here for dinner, then I would be here for dinner. Aunt Eloise was hands down the most frightening woman I knew.

I kicked the dirt off my boots with my walking stick and followed Emma inside.

"What time?" I asked, trying to gauge if I would have time to go into town after the guests left.

"They'll be here at six," she said. "And after that, they want me to play the piano for them."

"Of course they do." I tempered my response with a smile.

So there would be more paint drying tonight and I wouldn't be going into town after all.

3

MACKENZIE

Grandpa, apparently, had hired an assistant named Tracie.

As Tracie brought in a tray with hot tea along with some crackers and cheese, it occurred to me that I could use an assistant myself.

Sometimes I even forgot to eat. An assistant could help with that kind of thing.

"Have a seat, Tracie," I said, sitting in an armchair. "Tell me about yourself."

Tracie's eyes widened.

"Yes ma'am," she said, sitting on the edge of a chair across from me.

Classic type A personality, I decided.

"How long have you been working for Grandpa?"

"Not long," she said. "only a couple of weeks."

"And you live here?"

"Oh no ma'am," she said. "But if you need me to, I can make arrangements to be here more."

"Not necessary," I said with a smile. "What you and Grandpa have worked out is fine, I'm sure."

"I should go check on him," she said.

"Okay," I said. "Nice to meet you."

"Thank you," Tracie said, jumping up and leaving the room. "You too."

Tracie obviously had a lot of insecurities, but her eagerness to please no doubt made up for it.

Standing up, I walked to the window. The cat got up and walked with me.

"What's your name, Kit Kat?" I asked.

The cat didn't answer.

"I guess I'll call you Kit Kat then until I find out otherwise. Seems you're the only one who wants to listen to me at the moment."

Kit Kat just blinked and rubbed against my legs.

Looked like he wasn't really talking right now either.

The wind blew through the trees outside, sending leaves and moss scattering across the lawn.

Looked like Grandpa had let the yard maintenance go. Another sign that he was developing dementia.

A few minutes later Grandpa joined me in the parlor.

"I'm sorry, Mackenzie," he said. "I had to take that."

"It's no problem," I said, with a smile. "I'm in no hurry."

Not until tomorrow anyway. Then I would be ready to go. To get home so I could catch up on some work. Get ready for next week.

I walked over and sat back down on the sofa. Kit Kat followed, jumping up to sit next to me.

"When did you get a cat?" I asked.

"Last week," he said, sitting across from me. "Tracie and I went down to the pound and rescued him.

I quickly squashed down the little spurt of jealousy mixed with guilt that someone outside of family had to take Grandpa to the pound to rescue a pet.

When Grandpa patted his knee, Kit Kat ran over and jumped in his lap.

"I think he likes you," I said.

"He's my buddy," Grandpa said, rubbing the cat's ears.

"Good. I'm glad you have him."

"And I'm glad you could come. Is Victoria okay?"

"Yes. She's busy with work, as always."

"That's how it is with doctors."

Grandpa got points for remembering that Victoria was a doctor.

"So… as I said, I haven't heard from Cameron lately. I'm getting a little concerned about him."

"I'm sure he's good," Grandpa said. "I don't think he's going back California."

"Oh." Cameron loved California, especially his job. "What about his condo?"

"He sold it."

Sold it. That was a big move. "So he moved. Do you know where he went? Is he living here with you?"

"His car is here," Grandpa said, giving me that vague answer about the car again.

"Okay," I said with utmost patience. "If his car is here, but he isn't, how is he getting around? Did he get another car?"

"Do you want some tea?" Grandpa asked, not answering my question.

"Sure." Though truthfully I would have preferred a latte right about now. Something to stall out the headache I felt coming on.

"How often does Tracie get to come out?" I asked.

"Three times a week," he said.

"That's not very often," I said. "If you need her to come out more often, I can help with the money."

"I'm not hurting for money," Grandpa waved a hand, dismissing my offer. "Got more than I can spend. Ever."

"I see. So do you have plans to at least spend some of it?"

"I'll spend it on caregivers and on food and such. Doesn't take much to live."

I jumped onto clinician alertness. If Grandpa was suicidal, then I definitely needed to intervene.

"She and I are going shopping nest week for groceries. I don't drive anymore."

I knew that. We all knew that.

"Someone told me that," I said. "it's commendable that you willingly gave up your car keys." I really didn't know if he gave them up willingly or not, but I wanted him to think I knew that it had been willingly.

"I don't know about that," he said. "But it was time."

"Well, if you thought it was time, then I have to agree."

"Getting older is not for the faint of heart," Grandpa said, tapping his knee with the back of his hand.

"No, wouldn't think so. I just hope you feel good enough to move around and do what you want to do."

"I do alright," he said. "Having Tracie here to help out helps. Especially without Sophia or Cameron around."

"Just make sure you do your exercises," I said.

Grandpa nodded and I got a sense he was merely appeasing me.

I would have to spend more time with him to really know if he had dementia. Except for the way he talked about Cameron, he seemed to be holding his own.

I needed to back up and run at it again.

"When was the last time you saw Cameron?" I asked.

"Come on," Grandpa said. "Let's make something to eat."

4

ANDREW

The strains of the lively piano music filled the parlor. It had been nearly an hour now.

I maintained that it was like watching paint dry.

The guests my aunt and uncle had over were my brother Nathan and his wife, Sophia.

We rarely saw them, especially now that they had the baby.

Sophia bounced little Kenzie on her knees. The baby was fussy. Bored, I thought. The baby sounded like I felt.

Why we had to sit here to listen to my cousin play was beyond me. We could be up, having an actual conversation while Emma played the piano in the background.

It truly did not seem like too much to ask.

I'd already nodded off twice. Fortunately I sat in the back, making it hard for anyone to see me.

Finally, she stopped, stood up, and bowed.

Everyone clapped. I clapped, too, though I had no heart in it. Reminding myself that I was glad it was over, helped with my appearance of enthusiasm.

I slipped out the front door, grabbing a long black cloak

and a top hat on my way out, and walked along the path leading to the back of the house.

The bright glow from the full moon spilled over the magnolia bushes in full bloom and the smaller flowers growing among them. Roses. Daffodils.

Their intoxicating scents blended together smelled like an exotic perfume.

Out of sight of the house, I stopped and propped one foot on a wooden bench. I pulled a cigar out of my pocket and lit it.

Inhaling the earthy scent, I closed my eyes.

This was not my favorite way to spend an evening, but at the end of the day, my family came first.

I put my family's needs before my own. If I didn't, I would have stayed in New Orleans where there was a party going on every evening.

Clouds shifted over the moon, creating shadows over the garden. A dog howled somewhere in the distance, then a couple of dogs set off in a barking frenzy.

I blew out a stream of smoke, then kept walking, making a lap through the trees. As I came back around, walking toward the back of the house, I stopped.

Emma's music was already going again. The girl barely took a break from it.

But. It did not sound like Emma playing. And I would know with as many hours spent listening to her play as I had, I should know.

Emma always played bright, lively music. This music, however, was somber. I would have sworn it was my sister, Isabella, but she wasn't here tonight. She and her new husband, Cameron, lived in a two-story townhome in Natchez.

I didn't know much about Cameron except that he wrote novels. That and he made her deliriously happy. It was weird that she was married now. Isabella and I had always shared the opinion that marriage was not something we felt pulled toward.

Drawn to the somber music, I walked slowly up the back steps and cautiously made my way around the veranda to the window where the soft glow of candlelight spilled outside.

The first thing I noticed was that the room was empty. All the extra chairs had been put away and everyone had left.

I had not been gone so very long. Just long enough to take a short walk.

Then I saw the piano. A young lady sitting there, her head bent over the keys.

Surely it wasn't Emma. The music did not sound like Emma's.

I moved closer, pressing my forehead against the cool glass of the French door, and squinting into the dim light just as she lifted her head giving me a clear view of her profile.

The girl playing the piano was not Emma.

Emma always wore her hair pulled back.

This girl had long hair waving around her shoulders.

And her features. Mon Dieu. This young lady was the most beautiful woman I had every laid eyes on.

Even from here I could see her plush lips, slightly parted, her strong jawline, and her perfect nose.

Yet she carried a sadness about her.

Whatever it was about her, I felt like a bolt of attraction came down from the heavens and struck me with a magic love potion.

Even as a man who liked women, this was a foreign sensation to me.

I knew right then and there that I had to have her.

5

MACKENZIE

I sat at the piano, letting the music flow through me onto the smooth delicate keys. I hadn't touched a piano in ages, but it came back to me as easily as riding a bicycle.

I'd played in college. Even had a professor practically beg me to change my major to music.

But I'd been dead set on psychology. Then as I went through graduate school, I had less and less time to play.

Until now, I didn't even own so much as a keyboard.

But this old piano had always been my favorite. Built in the 1800s, it reminded me of a smooth wine, aged to perfection. Or maybe even a grand old lady, refined and regal.

After Grandpa and Tracie had put a frozen pizza in the oven, we'd sat at the kitchen table and watched Jeopardy on television.

I gave up on trying to get any information from him about Cameron.

I'd back up and come at him a different way tomorrow.

Cameron's fire engine red Maserati sat in the back yard, locked, and I had no idea where to look for a key.

But I knew that it was best not to press Grandpa too much. There was no point in aggravating him.

I just needed to see how he was functioning on a day to day basis. To see how he was handling his activities of daily living.

It helped having Tracie here. I could see that already. So many elderly people resisting having someone around to help, especially way out here where there were no neighbors. I was rather proud of Grandpa. He'd given up his car keys willingly and now he had willingly brought in someone to help him out.

After cleaning up, Tracie left and Grandpa went up to bed early.

Left to my own devices, I wandered around for a while. I'd walked around Cameron's car. Maybe he'd gotten another car. There had to be a logical explanation.

It wasn't like there was some kind of vortex that swept people away, never to be seen again. First, my sister Sophia. Now my brother Cameron.

Even as I told myself this, a chill went up and down my spine.

After that, I'd followed my nightly routine. Checked my emails, then set both my phone and my iPad aside for one hour. During that hour I had a glass of wine while I read a book. I did not read on my phone or even my iPad. I read actual books that I could hold in my hand.

I plucked at random from Grandpa's extensive library collection. I read everything. It didn't matter what genre. And with every book I learned something about the human psyche. After all, that's what a book was. One person's perspective on the world.

As humans, we shared our collective unconscious through books and movies… Through entertainment.

As both a professor and a psychologist, I often assigned movies to help people view emotions through a different perspective. I used them to education. I would assign books, but I had quickly learned that people were much more likely to spend two hours watching a movie than they were to invest time in a book.

After my hour of reading and relaxation, I usually went to bed.

But not tonight. Tonight I took my unfinished glass of wine with me as I wandered the house again. I traded my glass a wine for bottle of water. Stopped in the foyer to study the tall grandfather clock that stood next to the stairs. It stood silent as it always did. I slash across its face between the six and seven—a badge of honor earned during the Civil War.

Maybe I would look into having the clock repaired. Someone needed to. It seemed like the house would be complete if it were ticking again… chiming the hour. I'd heard it once when I was a child. It was definitely a part of the house.

Going into the parlor, I sat at the piano. Since Kit Kat had followed Grandpa upstairs, I was completely alone.

I lost track of time as I played, letting my emotions run unchecked. I needed to add music back into my life. I resolved to order myself a keyboard.

I stopped a minute to drink water, then played one of my favorite pieces. It brought to mind a mixture of love and heartbreak. After all, weren't they intermingled?

According to my clients, they certainly were. If I were to believe why they told me without saying it outright, I would believe that happily ever after was nothing more than a bedtime story.

I hadn't decided what I believed myself. I was reserving judgement.

But right now as the music flowed through me, I believed it. I believed that love was a special kind of heartbreak that only the brave dared to experience.

And I was not brave.

As I neared the end of the piece I lifted my head, blinking back the tears that welled in my eyes.

I turned toward the window as I played the last notes.

Though my fingers kept moving, my brain froze.

There was a man standing at the window. Watching me.

A tall, dark, and handsome man wearing a long black cloak and a top hat.

I should have been afraid. Would have been afraid.

Except that he looked more like an apparition than a dangerous man. He looked like he'd walked out of the past.

As I ended the song and the strains of the music lingered in the air, I came to a conclusion.

Grandpa might not be the only one who needed to have a psychological evaluation.

Perhaps I also needed to be evaluated.

6

ANDREW

As the music drifted through the air, the girl turned and looked in my direction. I saw the surprise as it flashed across her face.

She blinked, but her fingers continued to fly across the piano keys as she looked at me.

As the last strains of the music lingered in the air, I reached for the door knob of the French door and turned. It was locked.

I whirled around and went to the back door. It was locked, also.

Running a hand through my hair, I went back down the stairs and hurried around to the front of the house.

The ground was dry beneath my feet and the air had an unfamiliar scent to it. Fetid and earthy.

In the distance, a pack of dogs bayed at the moon and an owl flew away, seemingly disturbed by my presence.

The air felt heavy and damp.

Thunder rumbled in the distance and lightning flashed over the tops of the oak trees, tossing the gray moss about.

I crossed the front veranda and held my breath as I turned

the knob. It opened. I stepped inside and was immediately greeted by my cousin's happy, lively music mixed with the sound of the clock as it chimed the hour.

Crossing through the foyer, I stopped at the door to the parlor. Emma was sitting there. Happily playing the piano. My family was seated as they had been before I left them.

My parents. My brother Nathan and his wife. Their baby still fussing, but on her father's lap now.

My older brother, Grant, looking about as happy as I had felt.

My cousins. My aunt and uncle.

Everyone who had been here when I'd stepped out for a walk.

But the beautiful, sad girl was not here.

Aunt Eloise, seeing me standing there, wearing my cloak and hat, glared at me.

Mon Dieu.

I would no doubt incur her wrath.

Villars, the Becquerel butler, appeared at my elbow.

"May I take your cloak and hat, Sir?" he asked.

"Thank you, Villars." I handed him my hat and slipped out of the cloak. "for coming to the rescue as always."

He nodded once, then turned. Always formal, Villars stood tall and straight. He knew everything that went on in this house. And yet I'd never heard him gossip or say an unkind thing about anyone.

"Villars," I called, going after him, keeping my voice low. "Did you see a young lady? With long dark hair. Um... Sad looking. Playing a sad song on the piano just now?"

"No Sir," Villars said with a glance toward the window.

"Are you sure?" I asked, knowing that it wasn't possible. It was as though I'd looked through a window into another place. Perhaps even another time.

The girl had looked different. Dressed different.

"It's a good night for a storm," Villars said.

Turning again, he took my attire, leaving me with no choice but to go back into the parlor to watch some more paint dry.

I did not care that my family looked at me disapprovingly. I didn't care if my aunt's wrath rained on my head.

I had just seen the woman I was going to marry.

7

MACKENZIE

I stood up from the piano and walked to the French door.

There was no one out there.

I pressed a hand against the cool glass and watched the lightning storm as it moved in over the trees.

I'd been overcome by emotion.

Playing the piano again had been bittersweet. I'd allowed myself to contemplate for just a moment what my life might have been like if I'd done what my professor had begged me to do.

If I'd taken something I loved—an art—and pursued it.

Instead, I'd gone the safe route. My career as a psychologist was something I'd felt I could control. I had a timeline. I'd had everything mapped out from undergrad forward.

And I had gotten exactly where I'd set out to go.

A career in the arts had not been in my plan. It contained a much higher level of chance. And I knew that only a few people were able to succeed to the top. The uncertainty was unmeasurable. Something I had not been prepared for.

Piano was simply something I did because I loved it. Not to earn a living.

Only a few people were able to earn a living with it.

I knew that. I also knew that the only person I could count on was myself.

As an older teen, I'd watched my mother go through a divorce.

She'd floundered for a couple of years during that process.

Momma had never held a job. My father had taken care of her from high school graduation on. They'd married young and my mother had her first child young.

So she had no marketable skills for the work force.

Fortunately, she'd met my stepfather and he had set her aright again. I know that she loved my stepfather. I also knew that she was fortunate to meet him before she was lost.

I did not want to be like that. Ever. I wanted to take care of myself. Not to be reliant on someone else.

So I'd kept my head down.

Turning away from the window, I pulled myself back to reality.

Overcome with the emotion of the music, I'd imagined someone at the door.

For just a split second, I'd thought it was perhaps Cameron. That had been my gut response when I'd seen the man standing there.

But the man had definitely not been my brother.

I loved my brother dearly, but he was not as handsome as this man.

This man was fiercely handsome. He could have stepped out of a fairly tale. Or the depth's of a girl's imagination.

My imagination.

But there had been no one there.

Too restless to sleep, I took my MacBook into the library and settled down at the desk.

A little metal photograph was propped against the Tiffany desk lamp.

A photograph of a beautiful young lady, obviously taken in the 1800s… before modern photography.

Although it was faded a bit, I could see that she was beautiful. And in some ways—maybe it was the way she was dressed—she reminded me of the man I'd seen at the door.

I logged into my online class. Made a few comments on the student discussion boards.

As I worked, my thoughts kept straying to the photograph.

And to the man at the door.

Tomorrow I would ask Grandpa about this photograph.

It was kind of an odd thing to leave sitting out like this.

But then everything about today had been rather odd.

8

ANDREW

I slid off Lightning Bug and walked along the rows of tobacco plants, bending down to touch a leaf or a bloom. Looking for anything that wasn't right.

The earth was still damp from last night's storm and the rain had brought out more blooms overnight.

The flowers were white and light pink.

I liked the look of the soil. Rich and moist. Exactly what was required.

My family thought of me as being irresponsible.

I was not irresponsible. I did my work.

As the youngest son, I had fewer expectations. Perhaps they simply saw what they wanted to see.

Father had granted all three of his sons two acres of land to do with as we pleased. I chose to grow tobacco on mine.

My brother Grant was offended by being given just two acres. Justifiably so since he had been in charge of a whole section of land at our country home down by New Orleans. Grant was the one who had invested his life in that land.

Father assured us that more would be coming to us over the

next few years. He had not explained his thinking, nor was he required to.

My other brother, Nathan, had built his own textile mill on his piece of land and was already leaps and bounds ahead of the rest of us, but he'd lived up here longer than we had. He'd chosen to move here.

My brother and I had moved here out of necessity. Followed our father without question. My sister had been the one to grumble the most. She did not leave New Orleans by choice. Ironically, she'd met Cameron and gotten married.

Everything happened for a reason, I suppose.

I spent my days in my little tobacco field. Not exactly what an irresponsible man would do.

I'd hired a couple of workers to help me out, but I did most of it myself. Even with their help, I oversaw the whole process beginning with the seeds I'd planted back in November.

My helpers only worked a couple of days a week, so today I had my land to myself.

As I walked along the rows of young tobacco plants, my thoughts circled back around to last night.

By the time Emma had completed her piano performance and we had all been allowed to leave the parlor, the thunderstorm was in full force around us.

Nonetheless, I had gone back out on the veranda into the blowing wind and rain and looked in through the window. All I saw was the empty, dark parlor where Emma had played the piano.

The beautiful young lady was not there and there was no evidence that she had been.

It was most perplexing.

I'd gone back this morning and done the same thing again.

Looked inside at the parlor through the window.

But still. No young lady. Just a parlor with no one in it.

I was determined to find her.

I know I had not imagined her.

She was, however, exactly as I would imagine the perfect girl.

I liked the way she played the piano. She played with heart and feeling. It was different from the way Emma played. Emma played with a gleefulness that would no doubt appeal to many. But in my opinion, Emma needed more practice. Alone.

Not for an audience.

I could not tell anyone that, of course. It would be the height of rudeness. As family, we were obligated to be her audience. Especially when Aunt Eloise insisted.

My sister Isabella had no idea how lucky she was to live in town and not be subjected to my aunt's whims.

My trip to Natchez Under the Hill had not only been subverted, it no longer interested me.

With no more than just one glimpse, the girl whose name I did not even know—and did not know how to find—had turned my world upside down.

I pulled my knife out of my pocket and sliced off part of a leaf. Sniffed it. It was a little early to tell how it was going to turn out as a finished tobacco product, but it was exciting to see how the tobacco was going to be different up here than it had been down south.

Looking across the fields toward the house, I wondered for the thousandth time today who the young lady could have been and where could she have gone.

And again, I resolved to find out.

9

MACKENZIE

The next morning I stood at the window holding a cup of coffee.

Since I hadn't found any yogurt in the refrigerator, I had bread in the toaster.

It was nearly eight o'clock anyway. Almost too late for breakfast.

I hadn't been downstairs long and Grandpa hadn't come down yet. I knew why I'd slept in. I'd stayed up too late working. My brain had been much too unsettled to sleep. So I'd worn off my energy by working.

And yet, still, I'd slept fitfully. Having trouble sleeping was unusual for me.

I tended to fall asleep easily.

That was helpful since I was a morning person.

Not today though.

"Good morning," Grandpa said, coming into the room.

"Good morning," I said.

"You just now getting up?" Grandpa went straight for the coffeepot.

"Yes," I said. "I stayed up too late. Working."

"I get it," he said.

I leaned against the counter and considered.

After last night, I had a slightly different perspective on things.

This house had always carried a bit of mysticism. I'd sensed that even as a child.

I had, however, written that off as a child's active imagination. Now. Maybe not so much.

Perhaps I shouldn't have diagnosed Grandpa with dementia so quickly, at least not without more information.

"You wanted to talk to me about something," I said.

"I did."

My toast popped up.

"Want some toast?" I asked.

"Sure." Grandpa went to the refrigerator and pulled out a jar of strawberry jam. Set it on the table.

I put the toast on two plates and went to the table to sit with him.

Something slammed against the door.

I jumped. "What was that?"

Grandpa laughed. "It's just the newspaper. The newspaper boy brings it around back for me." He shrugged. "He seems to think I'm too old to walk out front and get it."

"An actual paper newspaper?" I asked, mostly just to give my heart time to settle down.

Grandpa got up, went to the door and retrieved the newspaper.

He came back, holding it up. "Remember these?" he asked.

"Yes. I do actually. But it's been a long time."

"I like the feel of the paper in my hands," he said, sliding back into his chair and dropping the newspaper out of the plastic sleeve.

"I'm the same way about books," I said. "I like the way a paper book feels in my hands."

"Ah." He opened the newspaper and thumbed through the sections. "We're kindred spirits then."

He handed me the lifestyle section.

I looked at him questioningly.

"You still like this section?"

"Sure. I'm just a little surprised that you remember."

"Ah, Kitten," he said. "I'm not so old that I don't remember things."

I hoped I did not look too guilty, since that was exactly what I had been thinking.

"Grandpa?" I said. "Can we talk about Cameron?"

"Yes," he said. "but first I have news about Sophia."

"Sophia?" Sophia had gone missing ten years ago. The case had never been closed by the police, but we had all accepted the worst.

10

ANDREW

With the sun dropping over the trees, I poured myself a whiskey and went to sit on the back veranda. I was there to watch the sunset, as least as far as anyone knew.

If I happened to wander over to the French doors and look inside, well then, that was no one's business.

I propped my feet up on the rail and watched a couple of the hound dogs run after a squirrel. They treed it and set up quite a ruckus.

It was cooler tonight after last night's storm. Certainly not cold, but bearable.

In a few weeks, the heat would be oppressive. Fortunately, there was usually a breeze off the river. Not like down south, but there was a breeze.

The door opened and my Uncle Samuel stepped outside.

He lit a cigar and leaned against one of the wide white columns.

"Not going into town tonight?" he asked.

"Not tonight," I said.

"You're a brave man," he said.

"How so?" I looked at him curiously.

"Your Aunt Eloise might decide we need to listen to Emma playing the piano some more."

I laughed out loud before I caught myself, then cleared my throat.

"I thought she was going to tan my hide last night," I said.

Uncle Samuel blew out smoke rings.

"She's not so bad. She just worries. And she especially worries about Emma."

Since I couldn't think of anything kind, I didn't say anything.

"I've been meaning to ride out," he said. "take a look at your tobacco crop."

"It's coming along okay," I said, grateful for the change of subject.

"I knew it would," he said. "it's a fine piece of land." He took in another deep puff.

"Your father and I are going over the plat," he said. "Trying to figure out how to best divide up the land for you and your brothers."

"Oh," I said. "I didn't know that."

Grant certainly didn't know. Grant was ready to have an estate to run. Like he did down south.

When that house had burned, Grant had lost some good workers. A couple of them had relocated up here with him. But for the most part, they had moved on to the next job.

He wasn't optimist about finding good help up here. Not that he had advertised yet.

"He wants all three of you to have some riverfront property so you can build your houses."

I nodded. My brother Nathan had already built his house. And he had riverfront property.

"Is there enough land to go around?"

"Absolutely." Uncle Samuel scoffed. "I thought your father

should have told you all about the land, but he was determined that he didn't need a dowry."

"My father was smart, though. He divided the land up between me and your mother. Didn't even tell anyone. We all thought he'd just given a small part to your mother."

"How did you find out?" I asked.

"He left it in his will. He wanted to make sure all his heirs were taken care of. Not just on my side."

"That was very kind of him."

"He was a man before his time, that's for sure."

My thoughts wandered back to the girl I'd seen last night.

Somehow the idea of building a house of my own had gotten tangled up with thoughts of her.

I'd always figured I'd have a house. And a family. But I could never get a good picture in my head of what that would look like.

But now I could.

Now I imagined that girl sitting in the parlor of our house. Children playing at her feet.

I shook off the thought.

I was a confirmed bachelor.

And she was like a siren beckoning me over onto the rocks.

11

MACKENZIE

An hour later, Grandpa and I sat around the kitchen table. The contents of a cardboard box spread out across the table.

Grandpa had gone upstairs and brought back a shoe box half full of papers.

He handed me a letter from Sophia first. It startled me to see her familiar handwriting. I still had handwritten birthday cards from her that I took out once a year on her birthday to look at. Reading things she had written was my own little way of honoring her memory.

I read the letter twice. The first time for emotion. The second time to analyze the meaning.

Dear Jonathan,

If you are reading this letter, then you know that I have gone back in time. It worked.

I so hope you found this letter. It makes me happy that you know I've made it to the past safely.

I didn't get to say goodbye and I'm sorry for that. But we talked about this and I know you understand. Still I miss you terribly and wish that you were here with me.

Please tell the rest of the family that I love them.

Take care of yourself and know that I love you.

Sophia

Setting the letter back on the table, I looked at Grandpa.

"What does that mean?" I asked. "It worked?

"It was behind the window pane."

"When did you find it?"

"It was only a couple of months ago," he said.

I looked into Grandpa's eyes. Trying to find an explanation.

"I don't understand," I said.

Grandpa sat back. Blew out a breath.

"Sophia went into the past. It was only a couple of days for her, but when she returned here, it was ten years later."

"You knew she went back in time? Ten years ago?"

He picked up his water bottle and drank deeply.

I had to be careful not to push him too much. So I waited patiently for him to answer.

"I suspected, yes," he said. "She stayed here with me for awhile. We couldn't tell anyone. The police… they…"

"They wouldn't understand?"

He nodded. "She didn't want them to put her in the mental hospital."

I smiled to myself. "That's why she didn't tell me."

Grandpa shrugged. "Probably you especially." He slid another letter in my direction. "Here's the next one," he said.

. . .

Dear Grandpa,

Nathan and I are married now and we have three children. Two boys and a girl. We have another on the way. Can you believe it?

I am so happy. When I'm not caring for the children, I sketch out house plans. I may never use them, but it keeps my mind occupied.

All my love,

Sophia

"She's married now," I said, after reading this one two times, also.

It didn't hurt quite as much to read her words now. The initial shock had worn off some.

"She went for him," Grandpa said.

"So she had a choice?"

"Not the first time. But the second time. Yes."

"Is there another one?" I wanted to just get it over with so I could absorb all this.

He slid what looked like the last one over to me.

I took a deep breath and read it. Twice. Then a third time.

Dear Grandpa and Cameron,

It took me awhile to figure out how to get this information to you. Now it just seems crazily simple.

I don't know if this will work to go back in time, but it worked to get me from the past to the future. I was going to try it, but I didn't have to.

By the way, Grandma Vaughn is the one who told me this. Here's what she told me:

Put the key in the clock. Then in the second between the lightning flash and following thunder, turn the clock back one hour.

I really, really hope this works. If it does, we'll see you soon.

Isabella and I are waiting.
Love you both,
Sophia

I TOOK A DEEP RAGGED BREATH AND LOOKED UP AT GRANDPA. IT hurt to swallow and had to fight to keep the tears from falling.

"Cameron, too?"

"Yes, Kitten," he said. "Cameron, too."

I pushed the letter toward him. I hoped to God there were no more of them.

"Cameron… and Sophia…" he said. "Both of them wanted to go back. Both of them found their soulmates back in time."

I wasn't even sure I believed in soulmates, but I didn't tell Grandpa that.

I pulled myself together. I would deal with the emotions later. As a psychologist, I'd become good at tucking my own emotions aside until I was alone.

"What else?" I asked. "there has to be more."

"Your Grandmother Vaughn was born in the 1700's."

"Wait."

"Hear me out," he said. "Her parents died when she was young and she went to live in a convent with nuns. When she was sixteen, they determined that she should be married so they sent her to America to marry a man who lived in Natchez."

"They knew this man?"

"No. But he was a colonist and the King had women in convents sent over to be their wives. The girls were called casket girls.

"After they arrived in America and made their way north, they were attacked by Indians."

I watched Grandpa as he told this story. I could tell that he believed it. Every word.

"Vaughn was the only one who survived," he said, staring into space.

"How? How did she survive, Grandpa?"

"An old Indian saved her life by making a rip in time. She fell through and landed in the future."

12

ANDREW

Fortunately for everyone, Aunt Eloise did not require us to listen to Emma play the piano tonight.

It was a relaxed, informal evening. Mother, Aunt Eloise, and Emma settled into the parlor to work on their needlepoint.

Father and Uncle Samuel sat on the other end of the veranda, talking business. Grant stood next to me on the veranda and we shared a bottle of whiskey.

"I hope you have a good tobacco crop," Grant said.

"It looks promising," I said.

While I chose to plant tobacco, my brother chose to go the traditional route and plant cotton.

It actually worked well because whatever he planted, he could sell to Nathan for his textile factory.

"So," Grant said. "What happened to you last night?"

"What do you mean?" I asked, swirling the whiskey in my glass.

"You looked like you'd seen a ghost."

I stared out at the garden, bathed in moonlight.

As much as I trusted Grant, I wasn't ready to tell him about what I'd seen. I wasn't ready to tell anyone.

"I'm already," I said.

Grant nodded.

"You know," he said. "I had my reasons for not wanting to move up here." He pulled a cigar out of his pocket.

"I know. You were busy running the estate. You didn't have time to come up here."

"That is true," Grant said. "But I was also wary of some of the things that I'd heard going on up here."

As the youngest son… and the one perceived as being irresponsible, my family did not always tell me everything that was going on.

I was often, in fact, the last to know things.

It didn't bother me though. I figured that if it was something I needed to know, they would tell me. Like when the house burned and we had to sell the townhome to pay some debts. Father told me when I needed to know.

"What kind of things?" I asked. He couldn't just say something like that and not explain it.

A man had to have his limits.

"I'll tell you what I know," he said. "But don't hate the messenger."

"Is it that bad?"

"It worked out well enough for Nathan and Isabella."

I lit the cigar and inhaled deeply. Whatever it was, obviously had something to do with marriage, since both our siblings were married now. Sophia and Cameron were siblings. As were Nathan and Isabella.

"Alright," I said.

"Sophia and Cameron are from a different time."

13

MACKENZIE

Time travel was not possible.

Not possible.

Not possible.

I held it together long enough to get out of the house.

I walked down the dirt road at the front of the house. This was what everyone called *the old road* since Grandpa had made a new driveway that traveled along what had been the service entrance back in the old days.

The old oak trees, hundreds of years old, were so huge that their branches dipped down toward the ground. They provided a canopy from the hot mid-day sunshine.

Silvery gray moss decorated the branches. As I neared the highway, a car with a loud muffler zipped past.

This old house… the old oak trees… the river… had all been here two hundred years ago. Yet everything was different now. Electricity… cars… cell phones.

Yet two of my siblings had chosen to go back to another century. A time when there was no electricity… no air conditioning.

Had they really believed that they had met their soulmates back in another century?

They had given up everything. My sister, Sophia, had given up a career as an architect. My brother, Nathan, had given up a successful career as a screenwriter.

Why?

Time travel was not possible.

Leaning against an oak tree, I pulled out my phone. Rescheduled my flight to Denver from later today to two days from now.

I could handle my online classes from here.

Then I checked my calendar and sent text messages to five clients letting them know that I was unavoidably detained. That I'd reschedule when I knew more. They all knew that I had gone home for a family matter.

It wasn't a lie. Finding out that your siblings had traveled back through time definitely qualified as an unavoidable circumstance.

I needed time to figure this out. If Grandpa was delusional, he was a genius to think all this mess up.

A grandfather clock. Lightning storms.

Soulmates.

He even believed that Vaughn had another husband in the early 1800s and might have even had children with him.

I could not even imagine what a convoluted family tree that must make.

Grandpa was a Becquerel and he didn't carry the spell. So getting right down to it, it was really a Dupre spell, wasn't it?

I was putting far too much thought into this.

If he was right, then everything I'd ever known was just… wrong.

Up until this point in my life, especially in my career as a psychologist, I'd felt like I had a fairly firm grip on reality. I was good at helping other people sort out what was reality in their lives and what was not.

If Jonathan had been anyone other than my grandfather, this would have been so much easier. I would have taken him to the hospital and, if necessary, place him under an involuntary hold.

I was licensed in the state of Colorado, not Mississippi, but most people would do as I asked out of professional courtesy.

But he was my grandfather and I did not want him to be labeled as mentally ill.

But even more than that, an even more pressing problem, was that I still needed to know what happened to Cameron. I'd accepted a long time ago that Sophia wasn't coming back, but to have Cameron disappear from here as well was almost too much to comprehend.

I needed time to do more exploration before I left here.

I could leave here with things as they stood.

14

ANDREW

The little white flowering plants sporting big leaves smelled like jasmine.

I walked among the plants, letting my mind wander.

The horn of a steamboat traveling along the river filled the air with deep mourning undertones. A flock of birds traveling north cawed as they passed overhead.

I replayed the conversation I'd had with my brother last night over and over. Linked it with the young lady who had played the piano two nights ago.

At first I'd thought my brother was daft or maybe even had too much to drink, but I knew Grant. I knew him well. I'd seen him in his cups and last night was not one of those times.

I also knew that he was quite sane. And very serious. He would never jest about anything, especially not something so serious as accusing both our sister-in-law and our brother-in-law of being from the future.

He didn't know details. Claimed he did not want details. But he knew.

He heard things and saw things.

Unlike me, Grant had a tendency to stay on the sidelines and people quite frankly forgot he was there.

Our mother described him as a man of few words.

I'd heard her say on many occasions that it was a wonder her three boys were so different. One driven to succeed, one fun-loving to a fault, and one serious to a fault. Then there was our sister. I'd always thought she was serious like Grant, but then up and married a man—possibly from the future—and moved to town with him.

I never would have seen that coming.

Grant claimed he'd heard there some kind of spell. There was a spell alright. A spell that led our proclaimed independent sister to get married on her own accord.

Now that I thought about it, both Cameron and Sophia had appeared suddenly without explanation and they both were a little odd.

I always thought they were probably from up north. People from up north acting different from people down here, after all.

We had some cousins who lived in Boston and I always envied their independence.

So I had the conversation with Grant in my head and I had the image of the young lady playing the piano.

I'd seen her. And I'd heard her.

I had no doubt about that.

What I did wonder was whether or not she was from the future.

If so, how had I seen her?

If she was like Cameron and Sophia, shouldn't she have traveled to this time?

I needed to clear my head. Tonight, I decided, I would go into town. Make a visit to Natchez Under the Hill. Find a willing woman and clear out my head.

All this talk of time traveling and spells was outside my comfort zone.

I was a simple man. I liked a strong drink. A good woman. A fast horse.

Oh. And a good cigar.

Come this fall, I would have my own tobacco leaves to try out.

Yes. A simple man.

With simple needs.

15

MACKENZIE

I sat at the desk in the study—the desk where Grandpa claimed Cameron had worked.

His computer was still there. I opened it up, but it was password protected.

I could not even get into Cameron's computer to see if there were any clues to his disappearance.

Crickets chirped and frogs croaked outside the window I'd opened up to let in some fresh air. I believed that keeping a window cracked at night was healthy so I did that, no matter if it was hot or cold.

There was a storm brewing. I could hear the distant rumble of thunder.

I took a sip of water and set the bottle on the desk.

Kit Kat ran into the room like something was after him and leapt onto the desk, knocking over my water bottle. Water went everywhere.

I hurried into the kitchen, grabbed a towel, and soaked up the water.

"Kit Kat," I said. "You are trouble, aren't you?"

Kit Kat just sat in the floor, all innocent looking.

I picked up the computer to soak up the water beneath it. When I did, I found a letter taped to the bottom.

I looked at Kit Kat. He just blinked at me.

"You're smart, too," I said, sitting back down and carefully removing the envelope from the bottom of the computer.

The letter inside had Cameron's computer passwords.

I opened the computer again.

My hands shook as I entered his password.

I didn't know what I expected to find.

Some note that he'd moved to Fiji to escape child support of a secret baby. Anything other than something so impossibly elusive as time travel.

Instead, all I found was copies of things he'd either written or projects he was working on.

As I scanned his computer files, the storm rolled it, bringing thunder and lightning with it.

The logical part of my brain told me that I would have to deal with his projects, but right now I just wanted to know where he was.

In exasperation and not a little bit of fear, I slid the computer aside and, lacing my hands beneath my chin, stared at the photograph of the girl.

The electricity blinked out on the next bolt of lightning.

The computer, running on battery, was the only light left in the room.

With the way it was angled, all I could see was the photograph of the girl, glowing in the light.

Using my phone as a flash light, I got up and found my way to the foyer.

I stood in front of the grandfather clock, staring into blank face, ripped across the front between the six and seven.

The broken grandfather clock that stood silent and had stood silent for over a decade.

Reaching up, I opened the glass door and put my hand on the key.

Put the key in the clock.

I put wrapped my fingers around the key.

Then in the second between the lightning flash and following thunder, turn the clock back one hour.

I waited.

Lightning flashed in through the window.

Lightly touching the hour hand, I turned the clock back one hour.

I did not hear the thunder that followed.

16

ANDREW

Once again, my plans were thwarted by Aunt Eloise.

She insisted it was time to watch paint dry again.

This time my brother and his wife managed to avoid the entertainment, so it was just me and Grant and the four parents.

If my life depended on it, I could not say what the purpose was of Emma having an audience, especially not such a small audience.

I sat and listened to what was supposed to no doubt be happy music, but it just grated on my nerves.

Mother and Aunt Evelyn sat doing needlepoint. Grant sat on a chair behind us, occupying himself with whittling on a piece of wood.

Unfortunately, I had not had the forethought to bring anything to occupy my hands. Besides, what would I bring? I didn't whittle and I didn't do need needlepoint.

I went over to the liquor cabinet to refill my glass of whiskey, taking my time. Moonlight spilled over the garden and lightning bugs sparkled as they took flight.

Except for the blasted music, it could have been a beautiful evening.

Swirling the liquor in my glass, I leaned back against the window.

It was too late to make the ride into town. It was just as well since thinking about the girl I'd seen through the window had become my favorite pastime, overshadowing any allure I might have to entertain myself with other ladies.

I knew Emma's music well enough to know when she was getting close to winding down.

As the last strains of the music hovered in the air, I did my obligatory clapping, knowing that Aunt Eloise would look over her shoulder. Which she did. Right on cue.

Then I slipped out through the French doors, letting the quiet cool night air wash over me.

Tomorrow, I promised myself, I would leave for town before Aunt Eloise had the opportunity to corner me. I'd just leave the fields and go straight there.

I should have done that tonight, but I'd come home to clean up first.

Leaning against one of the wide white columns, I took a sip of my drink, letting it burn all the way down.

It was good quality, but I just didn't have the taste for it tonight.

I was restless.

I'd planned to go into town, to release some steam, but Mother had asked us to keep the peace while we lived in Aunt Eloise and Uncle Samuel's house. I understood that.

But I was a grown man, for God' sake.

At the heart of it, none of that was what really bothered me. It was nothing I wasn't used to enduring.

Family came first. Even if I was as irresponsible as everyone thought—which I was not—I would still put family first.

One of the old Becquerel hound dogs—I believe his name

was Charlie—came up to the edge of the veranda and started barking at me.

"What is it, Boy?" I asked.

The dog turned, took a couple of steps, and barked again, looking back at me.

What the—?

I'd never seen a dog act like quite like this.

It was like he was asking me to follow him.

When I didn't move, he turned back facing me, sat on his haunches, and started barking again.

"Alright," I said. "I'm coming."

I set my glass on the wide wooden railing and went down the steps to the lawn below in the darkness.

The dog stood up, wagged his tail, and started walking again.

"Okay," I said, following the dog to the edge of the woods. "Whatever it is, I'm coming."

17

MACKENZIE

Instead of thunder, I heard piano music coming from the parlor.

I winced as the player's hands stumbled over a key.

Then my brain caught up. There was no one in the parlor.

Grandpa was upstairs taking a nap. There was no one else in the house.

Then, as I stood there trying to make sense of all this, the grandfather clock began to chime the hour.

It chimed two times.

The *broken* grandfather clock.

As the chimes faded away, the piano player continued to pound on the keys.

Pounding was an apt description.

Turning slowly toward the music, I faced the parlor, lit by candlelight.

A young lady sat at the piano. I counted four other people, a man and woman sitting together on one sofa and another woman sitting on a chair with a man standing behind her, resting his elbows on the back of the chair.

They were all dressed in antebellum attire. Formal jackets

on the men, long full dresses for the women. One of them wore a bright sky blue dress, the other wore one in light green.

Then I saw a man sitting by himself off to the side, his attention focused on something in his hands.

None of them saw me.

I felt like I was looking through a window into the past.

But there was no window here to look through.

A hallucination?

Moving over toward the stairs, I sat down.

Waited for it to pass.

What would I tell a client to do?

I would tell them it was probably a brief psychotic episode. A hallucination mixed with a delusion.

I took a deep breath.

It could happen to anyone.

A missing brother.

Grandpa talking about time traveling to the past.

So my brain put it all together to give me hallucinations. Visual and auditory.

Definitely full blown.

But it would pass.

It's not real.

It will pass.

And my brain would reset.

That was it.

I needed to lie down. Rest. Take a nap. When I woke, it would be forgotten.

Simple enough.

It could happen to anyone.

I stood up and walked up the familiar stairs. When I reached the landing window, I saw that the storm had passed and moonlight spilled across the lawn.

A man walked behind a dog toward the oak trees at the

edge of the lawn. Another person who wasn't supposed to be here.

I continued up to the second floor. Apparently the electricity was still out. I stepped inside the guest bedroom where I slept.

It looked different. The large four-poster bed, high off the floor, covered with mosquito netting. So high there was a stool to climb up onto it. A large leather trunk at the end of the bed.

A least my hallucinations and delusions were consistent.

When I did something, I did it right, I thought as I used the stool to crawl up into the bed covered with an unusually coarse wool blanket.

A tactile hallucination added to the mix.

Interesting.

I pulled the blanket up to my chin and closed my eyes.

Breathe deeply. Let it out slowly.

It will pass.

18

ANDREW

Turns out Charlie was a girl dog.

She led me straight over to a heap of brush just off the path and proudly showed me three newborn puppies.

"Look at that," I said, looking down to see what she had. "Charlie. You're a good girl."

Charlie settled down next to the squeaking puppies, looking rather pleased with herself.

"What do you want me to do?" I asked, kneeling down next to the puppies.

I patted Charlie on the head. "I'll bring you some food," I told her.

When I stood up to go, Charlie stood up, too, and whimpered.

She barked once.

"What?" I ran a hand through my hair, considering. "You want to take them home?"

She barked once.

"Okay." I knelt down again and one by one gathered up the puppies in the crook of my arm. They were so unbelievably tiny and fragile.

With the glow of the moon guiding my way, I carried the puppies back to the house, Charlie trotting along at my heels.

With my little group, I went up the steps to the far corner of the veranda and carefully set the puppies down on the floor.

Charlie barked one time, then settled in next to her babies and nudged them close to nurse.

I watched in awe at the whole thing. How Charlie was not only such a good mother, but she had led me to the puppies so I could bring them up here close to the house.

They needed a blanket.

Stepping in through the back door, I realized I had forgotten all about Emma's piano recital.

Her music filled the house. I slipped upstairs to the storage room and found an old quilt that would do just fine.

Taking it back downstairs, I grabbed some left-over chicken from the dining room, put it on a plate, and carried it outside for Charlie.

She jumped up and started eating like she hadn't eaten in weeks.

I sat there with her, picking up each squeaking puppy, one by one to look them over. They were perfect.

Eventually the piano music stopped and it was quiet except for the croaking frogs, the chirping crickets, and the coyotes baying in the distance.

I was of half a mind to take Charlie and the puppies inside the house, but Aunt Eloise's wrath kept me from following my instinct.

Satisfied that it was safe to go inside the house now without being confronted on where I'd been, I went back inside.

The grandfather clock began to chime the hour as I reached the foyer.

The legend, I decided, of the time travel was just that. A legend. And nothing more.

Exhausted, I climbed the stairs again, going straight to my room this time.

Without even lighting a candle, I slid out of my clothes and climbed into bed.

19

MACKENZIE

I always slept on my left side on the left side of the bed. It was just a thing I did. Otherwise I could not sleep.

Sometime in the night, I woke in complete darkness.

I was warm and comfortable. So comfortable.

Then my eyes flew open in shock.

I was not alone in the bed. Instead I was snuggled next to a warm, teddy bear of a man with a hard chest. His arms, wrapped securely around me. He smelled like a swirl of tobacco, something earthy, and… dog?

I was certain I had gone to bed alone.

But I was not alone. Not anymore.

I lay very still. Thinking back through the events of last night.

The clock. The key. The people in the house.

My delusional hallucination.

I had somehow fleshed out a hallucination. Auditory. Visual. And tactile.

And now the tactile part had most definitely taken on a whole new dimension.

This was a rare type of schizophrenia.

One so intricately fleshed out that it seemed real in every way.

But it's not real.

My mind was tricking me.

I closed my eyes and concentrated on my breathing. It's what I worked on with my clients. Taught my students.

It was supposed to work.

The man shifted, pulling me more tightly against him, my back to his front.

I was pretty sure he wasn't wearing any clothes.

Now I knew how John Nash must have felt.

The man starting by kissing the curve of my jaw.

It's not real. It's not real.

I relaxed. Knowing that he was bound to go away soon.

But he did not go away.

Instead, he trailed kisses along my jaw all the way to my ear lobe. Then he kissed me across the cheek, stopping just shy of my lips.

He shifted us so that I was lying on my back with him on his side.

The clouds drifted, letting in moonlight.

Opening my eyes, I saw a most handsome man. The perfect jaw. Perfect eyes. Perfect lips.

And the way he looked at me was spellbinding. He looked at me like I was the most beautiful woman in the entire world.

It was a magical moment.

Of course it was. It was my hallucination.

Everything would be perfect.

As he ran his knuckles across my cheek, I turned toward him.

This was my hallucination. And I could do whatever I wanted to in it.

It had already lasted longer than I expected.

But I'd wake tomorrow and it would all be over.

Hopefully…

I may as well take advantage of the circumstance.

I turned into him, entwining my fingers in his hair.

After a moment's hesitation, he crushed his lips hard against mine.

20

ANDREW

I was having the most wonderful dream.

It had to be a dream. Either that or I had died and gone to heaven.

The young lady I had seen through the door. The young lady playing the beautiful music on the piano.

Was right here in my bed.

I'd fallen into bed, exhausted, only to wake, finding myself with her wrapped in my arms.

She smelled like magnolia blooms, vanilla, and sweet lavender all rolled into one heavenly scent.

I'd woken with my lips pressed against her ear.

She'd turned into me, soft and warm…and willing.

If this was heaven, I never wanted to leave.

I kissed her cheeks, her eyelids, her soft kissable lips.

As our lips locked together, time ceased to exist.

I took her hands in mine and held them over her head.

Then I began to move against her. Slowly at first. Gently.

Then she did something that I did not expect.

She wrapped her legs around me and began to move with me.

How was this happening? She was obviously an accomplished young lady. She played the piano like an angel. Only a well-bred lady could do that.

With my lips on hers, I moved my hips in little circular movements against her core.

I forgot to think.

We said nothing. Neither knowing the other's name.

Yet we didn't need words. We spoke our own language.

A primal language.

The one that kept the human race surviving for thousands of years and would continue to do so into eternity.

When she came against me, I held her close, holding her as she quivered, then trembled, catching her breath as the explosion of passion settled.

I pulled her close to me, cradling her body against mine, using my hand as a pillow for her cheek.

I did not need to take my own release. Pleasuring her was satisfying enough.

It was as though she had dropped out of the heavens just for me.

How was I such a lucky man?

Her breathing evened and she went back to sleep.

I lay there, watching her in the darkness. Catching no more than glimpses of her in the intermittent moonlight.

It was such a relief to know that I had found her.

I was just dozing off when I heard Charlie begin howling. The howling was followed by the growling and yapping of another, maybe two other dogs.

My gut had been right. The veranda was not a safe place for her and her puppies.

I reluctantly crawled out of bed, tugged on my pants and shirt, and threw on some boots.

I had to take Charlie to a more secure place to bed up.

The barn. I would take the little family to the barn.

Before leaving, I bent over to kiss the girl on the cheek. She stirred, a smile crossing her lips, but did not wake up.

As much as I hated to leave her side, I felt obligated to take care of Charlie and the puppies.

21

MACKENZIE

I woke to the sound of birds chirping and a lawn mower running outside.

I felt… satisfied.

It took me a minute to figure out exactly why I felt so relaxed.

Then images of last night came back to me. I had been relaxing. Sleeping off a delusional hallucination.

It had most definitely been a fully fleshed out tactile hallucination.

The man had moved against me perfectly. Knowing exactly how I liked it. Rhythmic circular motions. I clearly remembered wrapping my legs around him and letting him take me to climax.

Why not? He had been my hallucination, after all.

A good way to wake up, even though I had promptly gone back to sleep right afterwards.

I pulled the other pillow over and pressed it against my nose. The unexpectedly intoxicating scent of tobacco and dog and something earthy was gone.

I turned on my back and stared up at the ceiling.

I'd gotten what I both wanted and expected.

I've woken up with my hallucination gone.

Now I was back to reality. The boy Grandpa paid to mow his lawn was outside, doing his job.

Definitely reality.

Unfortunately, reality was not nearly as interesting as my internal experiences.

I had a friend who was a nurse practitioner. I'd ask her to send in a prescription for Risperdal. I'd take it for a couple of weeks. Make sure the hallucinations did not return. I was pretty sure they would not.

I'd been under distress and when the mind was distressed—just like the body being in distress—strange things happened.

Brief psychotic episodes were usually just that. Brief one-time occurrences. So I was not particularly worried.

In fact, now I knew what it was like to have a full-blown psychotic break. It could only help me better understand the inner life of my clients who experienced similar things.

Sitting up, I put my feet on the floor.

There was only one thing that did particularly bother me.

I had fallen for a stranger that I had made up in my head.

As far as hallucinations went, I could not ask for a better one.

Maybe he would visit me again. tonight. Before I left for Denver.

I blushed at my own thoughts.

I was actually wishing for the return of a hallucination.

"What has gotten into me?" I asked of no one other than the ceiling.

Tomorrow I would get the prescription for the antipsychotic medication filled at a local pharmacy. Go ahead and start it. It would not do to have an episode on the plane going home.

I shuddered.

I still did not know what to do about my brother and his supposed travel to the past.

Might be best to just leave that alone for now.

There was still a chance he would show up. Still a chance that Grandpa had forgotten where he had gone.

Maybe Cameron had called an Uber to take him to the airport and he'd gone overseas to have a rendezvous with someone he met online.

It could happen. And with my free-spirited brother being like he was, it was actually more than possible.

I don't know why I had not thought of that before, but it was quite possible and Grandpa, in the early stages of dementia, had confabulated the whole time-travel story to help him cope.

He sat out here in this old house all alone, all day long. It should come as no surprise that he would entertain fanciful tales.

Intricate tales, I mused.

So intricate that he had somehow pulled me into it, however temporarily.

And however willingly.

22

ANDREW

The pack of wild dogs ran off when I went outside. I gathered the puppies up once again and carried them, Charlie at my feet, to the barn.

Fortunately, I'd thought to bring a lantern this time, so I could see well enough to find the puppies and their proud momma a safe place inside the barn.

I should have brought them here to begin with and we were fortunate that wild dogs had not attacked the puppies.

That guilt would have been hard to get over.

I tucked the blanket in a safe spot between two hay bales, then carefully placed the puppies on it. Charlie jumped right in, finding her spot nestled against her babies.

A good dog, I mused, and a good mother.

The thought, oddly enough, brought me back to thinking about the young lady.

In the morning, I would find out who she was and how she came to be here.

I wasn't sure I bought into the whole time-travel idea.

But what I did buy into was finding the one girl who sent my heart racing.

There was nothing else like that.

I might be a playboy, but at my core, I was a gentleman.

And as a result of being a gentleman, I decided I would not return to her room—my room actually. It would only make things awkward.

So I made myself a place to sleep in the barn, not too far from them. Besides, the puppies needed someone nearby to protect them. They probably were not even a day old yet and little Charlie could only do so much.

She was certainly no match for a pack of wild dogs. Not with puppies at her feet.

Before turning in, I took one more walk outside before bed, using the dogs as an excuse.

In truth, I wanted to look toward my window. To see some evidence that she was there.

But the window was dark.

Of course it was.

She was sleeping.

I wandered back to the barn and settled in on top of a hay bale.

I could have gone inside. Slept on one of the sofas. With my family here, all the guest rooms were occupied. Nonetheless, there were other options. Villars would know.

But I didn't want to go back inside the house right now.

I had too much on my mind.

I'd known a lot of women. Whether ladies or otherwise. But none of them had taken hold of me like this one.

I didn't know her name.

Didn't know where she came from.

Had never even spoken to her.

I replayed my conversation with Grant. The one about the time travel and the spells.

As a down to earth, realistic man, I didn't believe in such things.

But, being from New Orleans—the land of voodoo and other mystical things—I could not simply dismiss it out of hand.

That would not be smart.

And despite my reputation, I was pretty damn smart.

23

MACKENZIE

"I have to go into town."

Grandpa looked up from his newspaper.

"Okay," he said. "Do you need some company?"

Looking out the window, I tapped the warm coffee cup I held in my hands. It was a beautiful spring day. Birds were scattered about on the lawn, taking advantage of the freshly mowed grass.

The lawn boy had the blower out now. A comfortable and familiar background noise.

"I'm sorry," I said. It wasn't like me to lose focus. "What did you ask me?"

"I asked if you wanted company," Grandpa said, with a little smile.

I shook my head. "You can come if you want to. I just have to pick something up at the pharmacy."

Grandpa set the newspaper down.

"What's on your mind, Kitten?" he asked.

"It's nothing," I said. "Just all that talk of time travel and spells."

"I understand," Grandpa said, leaning back in his chair.

"Want to talk about it?"

Grandpa would have made a great psychologist. He had some good innate skills to work with.

"I don't know," I said.

Grandpa waited. Got up. Refilled his coffee cup and sat back down.

"Last night during the storm," I said. "I did the thing with the clock. With the key and the hands."

He hid his surprise well, but I didn't miss it.

"What happened?" he asked.

I took a deep breath. I was a private person. It was just one of the reasons why I was so good at what I did.

I was able to put my own thoughts aside and did not feel compelled to share my own experiences. Only on rare occasions did I tell a client anything personal about myself.

I trust Grandpa. He and my three siblings were the four people in the world that I felt I could tell anyone.

If I was going to tell anyone, it would be Grandpa.

But with Sophia disappearing from here ten years ago and his belief that Cameron had also gone back in time, Grandpa did not need any additional stress.

I was supposed to be helping him, not unburdening my own troubles.

I shook my head.

"Just my imagination," I said.

I'd never known my imagination was that active. Cameron was the creative one. The writer. My hallucination was something like Cameron could invent on the page.

But the human mind was an absolutely amazing thing. Mine had taken everything Grandpa had told me and swirled it into a fully fleshed out hallucination.

Maybe this happened for a reason. Maybe it would allow me to help someone someday who truly had psychosis.

"Kitten," Grandpa said, reaching out to pat me on the head.

"Yes?"

"Don't ever forget," he said. "You carry Becquerel blood."

24

ANDREW

After shaking the hay off my clothes and checking on the puppies, I made my way back to the house. I needed to bring some more food out for Charlie.

It was so early that the grass was still covered with dew. A couple of roosters crowed, greeting the morning sunshine as I walked through the garden, the flowers heavy with small drops of moisture.

At the scent of bacon and biscuits, my stomach grumbled.

I knocked the dirt off the bottom of my boots and went inside, going straight to the dining room.

My brother Grant was already there a full plate of eggs, bacon, and potatoes in front of him. As always, Grant was an early riser. Always up with the chickens. That's how he got so much done, I mused as I made a plate for Biscuit.

"You're home late," Grant said, between forkfuls.

I looked up at him.

"Late? It seems early to me."

Grant shrugged. "Early. Late. You must have had a busy night."

Grant was not a partying kind of guy. Very serious. One of the most serious people I knew, actually.

"Good morning," Aunt Evelyn said as she breezed into the room.

And there was the other most serious person I knew.

She swept her gaze over my disheveled clothing, landing on the heaping plate of food in my hands.

"Guess you're starved after last night," she said.

"This isn't for me," I said.

She and Grant both looked at me like I had two heads.

"You have someone outside?" Aunt Eloise asked.

"Yes. Her name is Charlie and she had puppies last night."

I turned on my heel and left them to it.

Geez. Must they always assume the worst?

I walked across the veranda, heading down the stairs to the barn.

That happened, I supposed. I'd let my reputation get ahead of me.

If I was going to settle down with the young lady I'd shared a bed with last night, I was going to have to fix my reputation.

It would not do to have her hearing things about me before she got to know me.

Whatever she heard about me would have nothing to do with her.

Nothing at all.

When a gentleman found the woman he wanted to spend his life with, he got himself reformed.

When I set the plate of food in front of Charlie, she gobbled it up.

I sat down and, while Charlie ate, picked up each one of the puppies and held them close. Charlie trusted me with her babies.

Maybe that indicated a step in the right direction toward reforming my reputation.

25

MACKENZIE

I shifted impatiently as I waited in line at the pharmacy. The little local pharmacy was busy today. Or slow. Maybe slow and busy.

Grandpa had ridden into town with me, but he waited in the car.

I'd ended up asking him to ride in with me. Tracie didn't come out until tomorrow, so he'd be there alone. Besides, he didn't drive anymore, so it was good for him to get out some. And since I'd be going home tomorrow, I would feel guilty leaving him home alone.

Besides, I enjoyed his company. We'd had a nice lunch at a little hamburger restaurant on Main Street.

Finally, I was next in line.

My friend, the nurse practitioner, had tried to discourage me from taking the medication. She'd never questioned me when I recommended medication for clients.

But she'd gone down a list of side effects.

I didn't want to tell her about the hallucinations, so I told her I was having acute anxiety.

She finally relented and gave me enough for two weeks.

"Picking up for Mackenzie Becquerel," I told the girl behind the counter.

"Sure." The girl tapped on the screen, then went to the back. "The pharmacist needs to talk to you," she said.

"That's okay," I said. "I'm familiar with the drug."

"I'll let the pharmacist know," she said. "You can wait over there."

So I had wait anyway.

Ten minutes later, the pharmacist, a stern-looking older man, came up to the counter and, peering at me over his spectacles, went down a list of side-effects for the medications.

I listened, purposely ignoring the stern way he looked at me, signed the acknowledgement, then escaped to the car.

"Everything alright?" Grandpa asked as I slid into the driver's seat.

"Just a really long line," I said. "Ready to head home?"

I navigated the traffic and finally made it to the highway.

I began to relax as we drove home.

"Do you like it in Denver?" he asked.

"It's okay," I said. "I mostly stay busy and don't think about where I am."

"You have to make the most of wherever you are," he said.

"That's good advice."

The road turned to follow along the river. One of the touristy paddle wheelers traveled out in the middle of the Mississippi River.

"You never talk about dating anyone."

"I'm not," I said. "Not right now."

"No need to rush," he said. "you'll know when the right person comes along."

"Thanks Grandpa," I said.

The right one. If there was such a thing. I'd certainly invented the right one for myself last night.

But that wasn't something I could talk to Grandpa about.

We rode in silence until we reached our long driveway.

"I thought I heard piano music last night," I blurted. "Have you ever heard it?"

"I heard you playing the other night."

The large trees with silvery gray moss, dancing in the wind, draped over their limbs created a canopy over the driveway. I glanced at the clock. Only five-thirty-seven and already it was getting dark. Another storm?

"What about last night?"

"No," Grandpa shook his head.

I pulled around behind the house and put the car in park.

"Cameron heard music," he said.

A tendril of something—fear perhaps—traveled along my spine.

"Piano music?"

"I think it was orchestra music."

"How do you make sense of it?" I asked.

We'd already talked about it. I guess I hadn't gotten the answer I wanted yet.

"I'd say you're being beckoned through the rip in time."

Maybe I wasn't the only one who needed medication.

26

ANDREW

After spending an hour or so in the barn with Charlie and the puppies, I skipped downstairs altogether and went up by way of the outside stairs to the second floor.

We rarely used the outside stairs. I wasn't sure why. It was just one of those things.

I was beginning to think, though, that using the outside stairs was a good way to avoid Aunt Eloise.

Maybe it was time to start thinking about getting my own place. Father was building a new house for the family, but Nathan and Sophia had their own place, as did Cameron and Isabella. I'd never given it much thought, but maybe there came a point when a man had to think about striking out on his own.

Reaching my bedroom door, I hesitated. If the young lady was still here, it would be inappropriate for me to barge in.

So I straightened my wrinkled shirt and ran a hand through my disheveled hair. With one hand on the door frame, I hesitated. Not exactly how I wanted to meet the woman of my dreams.

I could go to Grant's room. Take a bath. Get cleaned up.

That seemed like a much better option at this point.

I turned and came face to face with Villars.

"Good morning, Mister Andrew," Villars said.

"Good morning," I said.

"Can I be of assistance with something?"

"No…" I said. "I think I'll go to my brother's room instead. Take a bath."

"I can send up some bath water," he said.

"Thank you, Villars," I said. "You are a good man."

Villars beamed. How such a good man worked for Aunt Eloise was a mystery to me. But maybe it was just me she did not like. People usually took to me, but I suppose it happened.

Villars started to turn, then stopped.

"Something wrong with your room, Sir?"

"No. I just…" I shrugged, unable to come up with a response that didn't sound daft.

"I understand." Villars nodded. "It's a good day for a storm."

I just watched Villars walk away without a response. This was the second time Villars had made this same statement to me without any kind of explanation.

After knocking on my brother's door and not getting an answer, just as I expected, I went inside and started getting ready for a bath. My brother was in the fields. He was always in the fields any time he had the opportunity.

If the weather did not permit, he worked on his books. He was by far the most disciplined man I knew. Even more disciplined than Father, whose success was envious.

I thought about going down and helping bring up water for my bath, but they'd hired two young lads for that job and they didn't like anyone getting in on their process.

So I paced around the room.

Went through Grant's trunk and picked out something to wear. Grant had some decent clothes, but mine were better. Right now, anything would look better than the clothes I'd slept in all night in the barn.

I should have just gone back to my bedroom.

Restless. I was restless.

And what was it with Villars and his storms?

There was definitely a storm coming. I could feel it in the air.

27

MACKENZIE

I sat on the edge of my bed. A four-poster bed with no mosquito netting. Low enough to the floor that I did not need a stool to climb in.

A white down comforter draped across it. No coarse wool blanket.

Everything was as it should be.

I had everything packed and ready to go tomorrow.

I had mixed feelings about leaving. It was nice here spending time with Grandpa. But I had work. And I'd already gotten so behind with client appointments, it would take me at least a couple of weeks to catch up.

I held the little bottle of Risperidone in my hands.

How many times had I recommended this drug to clients? And they had trusted me. They had taken it because I recommended it.

I poured some of the little pills out into my hand. Then let them fall back into the bottle.

I recommended this drug to others for less than what I had experienced last night.

Yet I could not bring myself to take one of them.

Maybe it was my friend's reluctance to prescribe them. The pharmacist had looked at me as though something was wrong with me. I had seen the judgement in his eyes.

But that wasn't really what was keeping me from taking the medication.

As hard it was to admit, even to myself, I wanted it to happen again.

I wanted to see the man again.

No. I didn't just want to see him again. I wanted to kiss him again. I wanted to feel his body against mine.

I wanted to feel what I had felt last night. Again.

And again.

Maybe I could see my fantasy man again—one more time—before I went home.

Then if it happened in Denver, I would figure out what to do about that.

Was that so bad? To just want to be with him again?

I fell back on the bed.

I should take the medicine already.

How many times had I heard a client say they stopped their medications because they liked their experiences?

So I was a statistic now. No different from anyone else.

On sudden inspiration, I put one of the pills in my pocket and put the rest of them away.

If I found myself in the middle of hallucination, I could just take a pill and I would be okay.

Satisfied with my compromise, I curled up under the comforter and stared at the ceiling.

Rain splattered against the window. It was one of those long, soaking rains. Not a storm though.

I could go down and try turning the hands of the clock back, but without the lightning and thunder, that wouldn't work. Or at least it wasn't supposed to work.

No. I forced myself to close my eyes.

I was being ridiculous.

Just go to sleep already.

The episode had been a one time thing. It happened.

Just when I had my breathing at a calm, steady rate, the grandfather clock began to chime the hour, resonating all through the house.

I sat straight up in the bed.

This was important enough to wake Grandpa up for… to find out if he heard it, I decided, tossing off the cover.

I froze. My hands on the coarse wool blanket.

Sitting very still, I looked around me, but all I could see was mosquito netting.

28

ANDREW

About three o'clock a storm sent everyone running for shelter.

I ended up in the library with Grant.

"Whiskey?" he asked, holding up a bottle."

"Sure," I said over my shoulder. I stood at one of the windows watching as the rain came down in torrents. A rumble of thunder crashed around us.

Grant handed me a glass of whiskey.

"Thanks," I said.

"Is that my shirt?" he asked.

"Actually, yes," I said, glancing down.

Grant looked at me sideways.

"You ran out of your own clothes?"

"It's a long story." I swirled the liquid in my glass.

"Guess this weather screws up your trip into town tonight," he said.

"I wasn't going anyway," I said, letting the whiskey burn all the way down.

"What?" Grant made himself comfortable in one of the arm chairs. "Don't tell me you've taken a liking to piano music."

"Hardly," I said, with a glance toward the door. As much as I didn't like being a captive audience, I would never say anything to purposely hurt the girl's feelings.

That would just be uncalled for.

"What then?" he asked. "Lost your taste for the wild side?"

I laughed. "Maybe."

"Has someone caught your interest?"

I did not know how to answer him. The true answer would have been yes, but if he asked for more information, I would have been at a loss.

After bathing and getting dressed, I'd gone back to my room and nervous as a schoolboy, knocked on the door.

When no one answered, I'd slowly opened the door.

There was no one there and no sign that anyone had been there.

One of the housekeepers had come in during the day and made the bed.

I'd gone over to the chair by the window and sat down.

Now what?

Having not considered that she might not be here, I had no other plan past that moment.

"When are you going to have her over for dinner?" Grant asked.

"I didn't say there was anyone," I said, feeling a foul mood coming over me.

I should not have told Grant a damn thing.

"You didn't say there wasn't."

I glared at my brother.

"As the oldest son, aren't you supposed to be out there looking for a wife?"

Grant stood up and walked over to one of the bookcases, his back to me now.

"Don't worry about me," he said. "Everything is planned out. So all in due time."

I was about to ask him more questions. His response was much too vague to let go.

But Aunt Eloise came to the door.

"Oh good," she said. "You're both here."

Grant and I share a glance. We knew exactly what this meant.

"Emma has a new piece she'd like to try out. Don't worry. It won't take long and you can go on about your business." She waved a hand. "Whatever that might be."

Knowing it was not worth the fight, we took our glasses with us and followed Aunt Eloise to the parlor.

"Maybe next time," Grant said in a whisper. "I'll go into town with you."

"Right." I laughed.

Aunt Eloise glanced sternly over her shoulder.

I wiped the grin off my face.

What I did not tell my brother was I doubted there would be a next time.

29

MACKENZIE

Moving very cautiously, I left the bedroom and went down the hallway.

The ticking of the grandfather clock echoed through the house. Besides that, the only other thing I heard was the occasional murmur of voices coming from downstairs.

I hesitated outside Grandpa's door. Since the people in my hallucinations appeared to be quite real, I decided to hold off on that one.

Instead of Grandpa, I could very easily find someone else behind that door.

I wasn't in the mood to explain myself to anyone else or—even worse—for a confrontation with anyone—real or not.

Besides, I was curious to see what was happening downstairs.

It was dark, but I didn't mind moving in the shadows. It felt safer that way.

When I reached the top of the stairs, I nearly jumped out of my skin.

It was the piano again. Sounded like the same girl who had been playing last night.

It's not real. It's all in my head.

Holding my chin up high, I slowly made my way down the stairs.

Were hallucinations guidable? Like lucid dreaming?

Maybe I controlled what happened in my hallucinations.

Reaching the landing, I stopped. And waited.

The girl was hitting more wrong notes than she had last night.

I tried to ignore them.

Curious how long I was going to let this go on, since I might very well be controlling it, I decided to wait it out.

The girl did not play long.

Her little audience clapped, maybe a little half-heartedly.

I smiled to myself. Maybe she was actually playing well for her time period. It wasn't like people had televisions or computers.

Besides reading, they had very little entertainment.

I backed against the wall out of view as they dispersed across the hallway.

My hallucination. My way.

With all the people across the hall now, I continued down the stairs.

Once I reached the first floor, the clock began to chime again. I jumped.

Hadn't it just chimed?

Had a whole hour just passed? That quickly?

I stood in front of the clock and studied its face.

There was no rip in the face. No rip and the broken clock steadily ticked away the minutes.

I opened the glass, but there was no key inside.

I could not unhear the really bad piano music. I needed to get that out of my head. Really needed to get out of my head.

Slipping into the parlor, lit by only one lantern, I sat down at the familiar piano.

Did it look newer or was that my imagination?

I laid my fingers lightly on the keys.

Even knowing full well that it was best to not draw attention to myself, I could not stop myself.

I figured that if I was the one having this hallucination, I may as well do it my way.

I pressed one key, then another.

Then I lost myself in the music.

Closing my eyes, I let it spill through my fingers.

It felt so good to play again.

Just as it had the other day. Maybe better this time, now that I'd had a bit of practice now.

I moved from one song into another. This one a heartbreaking tune. There were no words, but I heard so much sadness in the notes that I had no doubt that it had been written about two lovers pulled apart by something out of their control.

My heart ached for them. Whoever they were. Even though I knew I was projecting my own thoughts and feelings onto the music.

As I played the last notes of the song, I opened my eyes.

A man was standing in the doorway watching me with hooded eyes.

He wasn't just any man, he was the man who'd made love to me last night.

A stranger.

But a stranger of my own invention.

I had not taken the medicine.

If this was any indication of how this worked, maybe I would never take it.

30

ANDREW

Tonight's paint drying session had not been all that bad, simply because it had been short.

Maybe one day I would find out why Aunt Eloise was so insistent that Emma play for us.

It wasn't like we couldn't hear her all over the house when she played.

I was in the library sharing a drink with my brother, Father, and Uncle Samuel when I heard the piano music.

Not Emma.

Most definitely not Emma this time.

It was the girl! The girl I'd seen through the door. And the very same girl I'd shared a bed with last night.

"Excuse me," I murmured to no one in particular, setting my glass on an end table, and leaving the room and the other men behind me.

Mother, Aunt Eloise, and Emma, also hearing the music, came to the door of the lady's study, but my father and Uncle Samuel both held up a hand indicating they should wait.

I strode straight to the door of the parlor before stopping.

I had been right. It was most definitely her.

She had her eyes closed as she played her heart out.

A heartbreaking tune.

One that pulled a man apart at the seams.

As she neared the end of the song, she opened her eyes and looked right at me.

It was almost as if she had known I would be standing here. Right here.

As the song ended, she rested her hands lightly on the keys and looked at me curiously.

"You play like an angel," I said.

A little smile crossed her features as she nodded her head ever so slightly.

Drawn to her like a moth to a flame, I walked toward her, only stopping when I was standing about three feet in front of her.

"Allow me to introduce myself," I said, with a small nod. "My name is Andrew Laurent."

"Andrew," she repeated, still staring at me.

"Your name?"

"Mackenzie," she said. "Mackenzie Becquerel."

Her last name caught me completely off guard.

Had my cousins been hiding her from me all this time?

"How are you related to my cousins?" I asked, not sure I really wanted to hear the answer. Some people had been known to marry their cousins, but the thought of marrying a first cousin was much too close for my taste.

"I don't think I am," she said.

"Yet you share their name." I took another step forward and rested my elbow on the piano.

"There are a lot of branches," she said, keeping her eyes—that I could now see were a lovely green—firmly locked onto mine.

"Then how are you here?" I asked. "You must have some connection to the family."

"It would seem likely," she said.

I heard someone at the door behind us. Glancing over my shoulder, I saw Emma peeking around the corner.

I heard my mother and Aunt Eloise talking in the foyer.

This was more than they could tolerate. They had to be in on everything.

"Would you like to take a walk in the garden?" I asked.

She tilted her head to one side as she seemed to consider.

31

MACKENZIE

As the haunting strains of the music faded away, I looked into the eyes of the man who had shared my bed last night.

He seemed amused by me. That in itself was a little disconcerting. Did he not remember the passion we had shared just last night?

A man that I created out of my imagination would most definitely have remembered.

John Nash's hallucinations remembered him from one incident to the next.

That was if I could believe the recountings I had read.

Maybe he was trying to keep things from being awkward.

Other people gathered at the door, peering at us.

"The garden." he asked, holding out a hand. "Come for a walk with me."

Taking his hand, I stood up from the piano bench and walked through the French doors leading outside into the moonlight.

"Will they follow us?" I asked.

"Not if they want to live," he said, leading me down the veranda to the gardens.

The gardens reminded me of how they had looked when Grandpa was younger. When Grandma was still alive and they worked outside together. It was one of the things they had enjoyed doing together.

The scent of magnolias and daffodils and roses filled the air, so strong it was almost hard to take a deep breath.

Andrew held my hand firmly as we walked down the path, out of sight of the house.

We stopped at a little wooden bench.

"Would you like to sit?" he asked, sweeping his other hand in the direction of the bench.

"Okay." I sat down. The bench was cold, reminding me that I was wearing nothing more than thin cotton pajama pants and a t-shirt.

Andrew, on the other hand, was wearing dress pants and a formal jacket.

I rubbed my hands over my arms, with a little shiver, mostly because I felt underdressed.

Andrew, without hesitation, removed his jacket and placed it over my shoulders.

He smiled at me, with a twinkle in his eyes that nearly took my breath away.

Inhaling deeply, I forced myself to think.

When I did something, I did it right.

Even hallucinations.

But, I assured myself, it did not matter because he was not real.

I was curious, though, about just how this delusion would play out.

"How long have you lived there?" I asked, already knowing what he was going to say. He was going to say his whole life.

"Only a year," he said. "This house actually belongs to my cousins."

"Oh. Your cousins."

"My whole family moved up here after a mishap with our estate."

"I'm so sorry that happened to you." I adjusted his jacket—that smelled like horses and dogs and something earthy—over my shoulders.

"It's hard to relocate like that."

"We're still adjusting," he said, blowing out a breath.

"You have a big family?" I asked.

"I have two brothers and one sister."

"That is a big family."

"Yeah." I studied his profile as he stared straight ahead. He was even more handsome in the moonlight than he had been in the shadows.

"In some ways it feels like it's getting smaller and in some ways it's getting bigger."

"How so?"

He picked up a rock. Tossed it away.

"My brother is married and they have a little baby." He smiled over at me, sideways. "My sister is married, too. She and her husband moved into town so he could write."

"Oh." The smile on my face faltered as his words tripped something in my brain.

"So he's a writer?"

"Yes," Andrew said, looking over at me. "He used to write plays, but now I think he writes books."

I flashed back to an image of Cameron's computer sitting on the desk in Grandpa's study.

This is not real.

It's not real.

32

ANDREW

I wasn't about to fill Mackenzie's head with all that babble about time travel.

In truth, I didn't want to talk about anything but her.

I didn't know how she was here, but some things were not meant to be questioned.

It was a beautiful evening bathed in moonlight.

The scent of flowers filled the air. The white night-blooming jasmine were my favorites.

Mackenzie was a lady and deserved to be courted as such.

I grabbed my knife out of my pocket and, reaching behind me, snipped a pink rose off a bush.

I put away my knife and presented the rose to Mackenzie.

Her eyes widened in surprise as she reached for it.

Our fingers brushed, reminding me of last night and the way our bodies had melded together.

I'd taken liberties with her last night. If her brother or father found out, they would rightly defend her honor.

I would, however, happily wed her.

So in the meantime, I would court her properly. Learn

everything I could about her. And woo her to the best of my ability.

If, perchance, she allowed me to steal another kiss, then I would not object.

"What do you do here?" she asked.

"I grow my own tobacco," I said. "I brought seeds with me from south Louisiana that I'm planting here. I'm curious to see how they turn out here in this northern soil—"

"Northern?" She bit her lip. "Here?"

"Why, yes," I said. "My parents moved to New Orleans shortly after they got married."

"But your house burned?"

"Yes," I said. "But… how did you know that?"

"I don't know." She looked a bit surprised. "You said there was a mishap with your estate that forced your family to move. A fire is what came to mind. That's all." She smiled a little.

Mackenzie was intelligent. I liked that.

"Where are your parents?"

Pressing the flower against her cheek, she made a face.

"My mother lives in France with my stepfather and my father lives in Washington with his new wife."

Mon Dieu.

She talked of divorce as though it was a normal, everyday occurrence.

But divorce was scandalous and no one in polite society spoke of it.

I kept my thoughts to myself.

"You have brothers?" I asked, deftly moving away from her parents' marital state.

A shadow crossed her features, though it could have been a trick of the moonlight.

"I have one brother. He's the oldest of the four of us, but…"

She stopped, not saying anything else.

Unable to stand seeing the pain etching across her features, I held out my hand for hers.

Looking at me with a little smile, she placed her hand in mine.

"Since your father is unavailable," I said, lightly kissing the back of her fingers. "I'd like to ask your brother's permission to court you."

33

MACKENZIE

My brother's permission? To court me?

An owl landed on a tree limb somewhere above us, rustling the leaves as it settled in. I never spent much time outside. Most of my friends and cohorts went mountain skiing and hiking on a regular basis, but I had a tendency to prefer staying inside. Always had.

Still. It was quite romantic sitting out in the moonlight next to Andrew. The mournful wail of a steamboat whistle in the distance. Beautiful fragrant flowers all around us.

The light pink rose bud on a long stem, he'd handed me was so beautiful… so delicate… and so unexpected.

The owl hooted and I jumped, stabbing my finger with one of the thorns and I dropped the rose.

"Ouch." I stuck my injured finger in my mouth.

"What happened," he asked, bending over to pick up the flower. "A thorn?"

"I nodded."

"Let me see." He set the rose across his own lap.

I hesitated.

"Come on," he said.

I held out my hand and he examined it.

"There's no blood," he said. "But it hurts like the devil, doesn't it?"

"It does," I said, trying not to pout. Normally a strong, independent woman, something about Andrew had me feeling like I could be vulnerable if I wanted to be.

He ran his thumb over the area where the thorn had stuck me, ever so lightly at first, then increased the pressure.

My finger didn't hurt anymore, but his touch was waking up all my senses and sending a coil of tension to my core.

When a dog howled somewhere behind us, Andrew looked up, alarmed.

"Come with me." He stood suddenly, bringing me with him.

"Where?" I asked on a little laugh.

"I want to show you something."

"That's rather mysterious," I said, but I followed him to the barn.

I tried to figure out where my unconscious mind had gotten all this stuff.

I'd never had a boyfriend lead to the barn to make out and I could not remember ever imagining it, either.

I was more of a go out to dinner and a movie kind of girl.

Nonetheless, I was intrigued.

I had never seen this barn before.

It was a large two-story wooden building. Weathered wood. A tall steeped roof.

We stepped inside through one of the large double doors into a large room with about two dozen stalls along either side.

From what I could see, the stalls had horses in them.

There was a buckboard wagon. A carriage. And a buggy. Lots of tack along the walls.

Tall stacks of hay lined the back wall.

That's where Andrew led me. Back to the hay.

I was just about to stop. Surely he wasn't planning a romp in the hay.

Then I heard the whimper of puppies.

34

ANDREW

The howling dog had reminded me of Charlie and the puppies.

Suddenly compelled to make sure they were safe, I'd brought Mackenzie with me.

The puppies were making quite a squealing, whimpering racket by the time we got to the hay stacks.

Stopping at the door, I quickly lit a lantern, then led Mackenzie behind the stacks of hay to the safe little cubby hole where I had left Charlie and family.

The puppies were there, but Charlie was not.

Mackenzie looked past me.

"Puppies," she said. "ducking under my arm to kneel next to them.

She scooped up the noisiest one and held him close, gently stroking him until he quieted. Then she did the same to the next one.

"You have a magic touch," I said.

She glanced up at me with a little smile. "Not really," she said. "I just love animals."

"Me too," I said.

She looked so vulnerable. So sweet. Holding the third puppy close.

"Where's the mother?" she asked.

"Not sure," I said. "I need to go to the house and get some food for her."

I hesitated. Did I want to leave her here or take her with me?

"Do you want to go?" I asked. "Or stay here?"

"I'll just wait here," she said. "Keep them calm."

"Okay," I stood up, reluctant to leave her now.

She was making cooing noises at the puppy.

Now I didn't want to leave her.

She turned and looked up at me with her big eyes.

"I'll be okay," she said.

"I'll leave the lantern," I said, setting it down next to her.

I left her, walking into the darkness.

Fortunately, I knew my way through the barn.

I closed the barn door behind me and hurried toward the back door of the house.

There would be scraps there for Charlie.

I stepped in through the back door and nearly ran right into Aunt Eloise.

"I need to talk to you," she said.

"I can't right now," I said, going to step around her.

She moved to block me, so I stopped and crossed my arms.

"I'm kind of in a hurry," I said.

"I don't even want to know," she said, rolling her eyes.

"I just need some scraps to feed the dog."

"The one with the puppies?"

"That's right," I said, wondering how she knew that.

"It can wait," she said, turning toward the library, obviously expecting me to follow.

So I did.

Even though I was in a hurry to get back to Mackenzie, I followed Aunt Eloise into the library.

"Sit," she said.

When I didn't sit, she shot me a look that had me sitting down.

"I need to talk to you about the girl."

"What girl?" I asked.

Aunt Eloise shook her head.

"You know perfectly well what girl. What is her name?"

"If you don't know—"

"Her name," Aunt Eloise said.

"Mackenzie Becquerel."

Aunt Eloise nodded.

"Has she told you where she's from?" she asked.

Had she?

"I didn't ask."

"It won't do you any good," she said. "Mackenzie is from the future."

Here we go. Talking about the time travel and the spell again.

"I don't care," I said.

"Not yet."

"What are you saying?"

She'd dragged me in here. The least I could do was to hear what she had to say.

35

MACKENZIE

Andrew had been gone too long.

I didn't have a clock or a watch or anything of that nature that would tell me what time it was. I'd come out in nothing but my pajamas.

Fortunately I had Andrew's jacket to keep the chill off.

Using light from the glow of the lamp, I watched the puppies sleep. I'd never had puppies so I was no expert, but they seemed restless. Probably missing their mother.

The horses were quiet, overall, just an occasional neigh or whinny. I leaned back and, after getting stabbed in the back with a needle of hay, decided that leaning back wasn't such a great idea.

I tried counting to ten. Six times.

Another minute had passed.

I had a pretty ingrained sense of how long fifty minutes lasted.

My sessions with clients lasted fifty minutes. When I taught face-to-face classes, they last fifty minutes.

Seemed like my whole work life was broken down into fifty-minute sessions.

A few minutes longer and I knew I had been waiting for fifty minutes.

Picking up the lantern and taking it with me, I left the safety of the hay stack.

The empty barn looked a whole lot different than it had when I'd been with Andrew.

It looked... lonely.

I knew I was projecting. The barn wasn't lonely, I was feeling lonely.

But since I was alone, that was normal and did not bother me so much.

What did bother me was that I was outside. Alone. In a world that I really did not understand.

I didn't know if I was in the middle of a hallucinatory delusion or if I was in the 1800s. I wasn't quite sure which one would be better. Or worse.

Either I had time traveled to the past and met Andrew or I had invented him as part of a hallucinatory delusion.

Reaching the barn door, I opened it and stepped outside into the darkness.

The moonlight was behind the clouds now, so I had to rely solely on the meager light from the lantern to find my way back to the house.

I really did not even know which way to go to find the house.

I stood still a moment, waiting for inspiration.

Some people had dead reckoning for finding their way around in the woods, but I did not. If I were in the mall, however, I could have found my way around without any problem.

That ability to find my way around the mall was doing me absolutely no good at this moment.

All I could do was to pick a path and follow it.

I should never have stayed here without Andrew.

I'd forgotten where I was for a moment. For just a moment, lost in the world of Andrew and the puppies, I'd felt normal.

He would run to the house, grab some food, and come right back. No big deal.

But something had happened. Something had happened to detain him.

Either that or my hallucination had expired and now I was out in the woods. Alone.

If that were the case, no one knew where I was.

Grandpa certainly would not know where to find me.

I could be one of those people who wandered off in the night never to be heard from again.

I froze.

Right there on a path to nowhere.

Just like Sophia.

36

ANDREW

Aunt Eloise went to the little writing desk in the library and opened the top drawer on the right.

She pulled out a letter and handed it to me.

"What is this?" I asked.

"It's a letter."

"I have to get back," I said. "Mackenzie is in the barn. Waiting for me."

"She can wait a minute longer," Aunt Eloise said. "I need you to read this."

Aggravated. Worried about leaving Mackenzie alone in the barn, I quickly unfolded the letter and held it close to the nearest candle.

Dear Jonathan,

I looked up from the letter.

"What is this?" I asked. "I don't have time for games Aunt Eloise."

"It's not a game," she said. "Just read it."

"No." I refolded the letter, strode to the desk, and stuffed it back into the top right-hand drawer.

"When I get back from feeding Charlie," I said. "When I have Mackenzie safely back here in this house, then I will read the letter."

Turning on my heel, I left Aunt Eloise there in the library. I stopped by the dining room, but everything had already been put away for the night.

This was going to require a trip outside to the detached kitchen.

But I had no time for that. I would get the dog something to eat after I retrieved Mackenzie from the barn.

I should never have left her there alone.

A woman should never be left outside alone, especially not after dark.

So many things could go wrong. She or even Charlie could knock the lantern over and the barn could catch on fire.

She could leave the barn and get lost in the woods.

She could be set upon by wild animals. Mon Dieu. There could be a snake in the barn.

I'd never been a nervous person. I'd spent my life pretty much not having to worry about anyone or anything other than myself.

I'd never been *responsible* for another person.

But now that I had Mackenzie, I was. I was responsible for her.

If something happened to her, I would never forgive myself.

I'd let Aunt Eloise waste too much of my time as it was.

I dashed out the back door and jogged toward the barn.

She would be alright. She'd know to stay there. To wait for me. She'd know that it would not be safe to wander around in the night alone.

She's from the future. I wanted to block Aunt Eloise's words from my mind, but they were there and I struggled to push them away.

She was not from the future. She was a Becquerel.

A cousin of some sort. A distant relative.

I did not want her to be too closely related.

That would not do.

I liked her too much.

And if I found that she was my first cousin, I did not know what I would do.

Reaching the barn, I threw open the door, and stepped inside.

It seemed so quiet. And I did not see a glow of light coming from the haystack. I left the door open to guide my way.

Yet when I rounded the corner of the hay stack, and looked at the area where Mackenzie should have been, I knew that she was not there.

Charlie was there. I couldn't see her, but she barked once in greeting.

"Sorry, Girl," I said. "I don't have anything to give you right now. I'll be back."

With fear stabbing my heart, I turned around and dashed from the barn.

Would Mackenzie know which way to go? Would she know how to find the house?

Of course she would, I assured myself.

Even my sister, who never went outside after dark, would know that.

Forcing myself to stay calm, I followed the path back to the house.

About halfway there, I stopped. If she had come this way, I would have passed her on my way to the barn.

Damn it.

I turned around and retraced my steps.

I would find her.
If it was the last thing I did, I would find her.

37

MACKENZIE

Just like Sophia.

The thought echoed in my head as the house came into view.

With relief flooding through me that I had found my way back in the darkness, I went up the steps onto the back veranda.

I dropped into the nearest wooden rocking chair and carefully set the lantern on the floor in front of me.

It would not do for me to set the house on fire out of carelessness.

As I sat there, rocking gently, I studied the flames inside the lantern.

The flames looked real. Leaning forward, I placed a hand flat on the glass of the lantern.

The heat felt real.

I'd bet money that they were real.

I'd bet money, but I would not bet my life.

At this point, I really did not know anything for sure.

I may have invented this entire thing.

I leaned back and continued to rock in the rocking chair.

My full-blown hallucinations were not uncommon. That's exactly why I had gotten medication for myself.

In fact… I felt inside my pocket and wrapped my fingers around the little pill I had tucked into my pocket earlier.

I should take the medication. That is what I would tell any client going through this.

Take the medication.

If I took the medication and Andrew went away, then I would know that he was a delusion and I had invented the whole thing.

I needed to know that. It would not do to knowingly crush on a hallucination.

It would also not do to crush on a man from the past.

Where was Sophia?

If I was actually in the past—which I was certain I was not —then would I find Sophia here? And perhaps Cameron, too?

Andrew had told me that his sister married a writer.

A man who had written plays.

Cameron was a screenplay writer.

Telling people from the 1800s that he wrote plays would have been logical. No one would know what a screenwriter was. But they would have known what a playwriter was. It would also follow that Cameron would start writing novels. He'd always talked about it.

But the screenwriting had always been too lucrative to stop. He'd fallen into it by accident to begin with. Then the money had locked him in.

But if he were in the past, then writing novels would come natural to him.

Wishful thinking, that's what this was.

I was doing what Grandpa had done.

I had invented a way to keep them alive in my head.

If my siblings had gone into the past, then they were still alive.

It was insanity.

But that the thing about the brain. It found ways to adapt.

Finding the back door open, I went inside, found a pitcher of what I hoped was fresh water, and filled a glass.

Holding the glass of water in one hand, I stared at the pill in my other hand.

I'd wanted it. I'd believed that it could stop the hallucinations and delusions.

After a quick shake of the head, I swallowed the pill.

I'd let this go on too far.

I went into the library and dropped into an armchair.

I was supposed to fly out tomorrow. But I was in no condition to fly out like this.

How was I even supposed to get to the airport if there were no cars in my world?

Leaning my head back against the chair I closed my eyes and waited for the medication to take effect.

Yes, I argued with myself. It takes several days or even weeks for the medication to take effect.

But if determination had anything to do with its effectiveness, it should work shortly.

I would just sit here for a bit and wait.

I had a plane to catch tomorrow.

38

ANDREW

The sun was up by the time we gathered back at the barn. We'd started at the barn, so that's where we'd agreed to meet at seven o'clock.

They were giving up. Grant, Father, and Uncle Charles. And the half a dozen workers who lived on the property who had been recruited to join the search.

As the mist began to burn off the river and the flowers opened up to the sunlight, I could see in their eyes that they were giving up.

I did not blame them. Not really. When I backed up and looked at the situation objectively, I knew I would have thought the same way if I were in their shoes.

They had given it a valiant effort.

I could ask for no more.

"Thank you," I said. "For helping me search."

With that, I turned and walked back toward the house.

They may be defeated, but I was not.

I would get a couple hours sleep, then I would start again. The sun, shining brightly, blinded me.

"Wait," Uncle Samuel called, catching up with me. "There are other possibilities."

I glanced at him, but kept walking. I was not in the mood to hear his theories about time travel or spells or whatever.

All I knew was that Mackenzie had gone missing. And I could not find her.

"Andrew." Uncle Samuel put a hand on my arm. "Your Aunt Eloise has a letter you need to read."

"I know." I kept walking. "She told me."

"Read it," he said. "It might help you find Mackenzie."

I stopped and looked at my uncle.

"Alright," I said. "Fine. I'll read it."

He let me go then. I stormed through the back door and went straight for the library.

I'd just read the damn letter. It wouldn't make any difference though.

I was in the library before my eyes had time to adjust to the dim light.

I went straight to the desk and pulled the damn letter from the right-hand drawer.

As I unfolded it, something to my right caught my attention.

I turned and gaped.

Mackenzie sat curled up in the chair. Asleep.

"Mackenzie," I said, going to kneel in front of her.

She slowly opened her eyes, then put her fingertips lightly against my cheek.

"You're real," she said.

I smiled. "Yes. I am real."

She smiled back and my heart melted into a thousand pieces.

I sat back on my haunches.

"Have you been here all night?" I asked. "We've been looking everywhere for you."

"Oh." Confusion crossed her features. "I just thought…" She shook her head. "You do look tired."

"A little," I said. I was exhausted. But overcome with relief that she was safe and well.

"Can I get some water?" she asked.

"Sure." I looked over my shoulder. There was a water pitcher and glasses on the liquor cabinet by the door.

"Be right back," I said, taking her hand and kissing the palm.

I got up and took two steps toward the liquor cabinet.

"Do you want—?" I asked as I turned back to look at her.

Whatever I was going to ask her left my brain.

The chair where she had been sitting was empty.

Mackenzie was gone.

39

MACKENZIE

I gripped the arms of the chair and slowly put my feet on the floor.

The house was quiet. And cool.

The air felt different. Drier.

Air conditioning.

Nathan had been here. He had said something to me.

Then I had blinked and he was gone.

Just like that.

My brother Cameron's computer sat on the desk. The metal photograph of the girl propped against the lamp.

When I woke, my mouth had been dry… from the medication.

I'd sent him for a glass of water.

And he had disappeared.

He had searched for me all night.

How was it that he had missed me? Had I walked right past him?

It was quite possible that we had somehow crossed paths in the darkness.

My thinking was a bit fuzzy. Maybe from the medication.

That was it. I'd taken the medication.

But… it did not work that fast.

Not at all.

It took days at best, usually weeks to work.

I got up and walked across the hall to the kitchen.

Grandpa looked up from his newspaper.

"Good morning, Kitten," he said.

"Hi." I went to the table and dropped into the chair across from Grandpa.

"You feel okay?" he asked, setting aside the newspaper.

"I don't know." I looked into his kind eyes. Grandpa knew all about time travel and spells and… "Did you ever see Grandma Vaughn disappear?"

"Yes." Grandpa's eyes narrowed. "You went back in time."

"Maybe." I rubbed my eyes with my fingertips. "I don't know."

He pushed his chair back.

"I need to show you something." He motioned for me to follow him back into the library.

Going to one of the shelves, he shoved books aside and pulled out a huge heavy book. A Bible and placed it on the desk with a loud thump.

"What is this?" I asked, standing next to him.

"It's the family Bible."

"I haven't seen this before."

"I keep it hidden." Grandpa opened it up to the middle. "I don't want someone to just accidentally see it."

"Okay." I shoved my hair back and looked down at where he was pointing.

The page he showed me was rather messy.

It had arrows pointing here and there.

Sophia Becquerel. Nathan Laurent.

Cameron Becquerel. Isabella Laurent.
Mackenzie Becquerel. Andrew Laurent.
Victoria Becquerel. Grant Laurent.

"What is this?" I asked, dropping into the chair behind me and looking at up Grandpa.

"It's the family tree," he said. "From the 1850s."

"I don't understand."

Not only were my siblings' names there, but my name was listed there. Next to Andrew's.

"All four of you," Grandpa said. "Go back in time." He looked at me over his glasses.

"No," I said, shaking my head. "That isn't possible."

"Sophia and Cameron have already gone back."

"It's not possible," I said.

"It is possible," Grandpa said, but I wasn't listening.

I could barely even think, much less hear him what he was saying.

Why would my siblings and I all be born in the twenty-first century only to go back in time to spend the rest of our lives?

"That doesn't make any sense," I said, mostly to myself.

"It doesn't have to make sense, "Grandpa said. "It's destiny."

I looked at him then. Looked right at him.

And the realization sank in that it didn't have to make sense.

40

ANDREW

I backed up and dropped onto the sofa, my mind numb.

A rooster crowed outside, reminding me that this day had not even gotten started good.

The scent of bacon filled the air, making me queasy. The men would be on their way in for breakfast. We'd had coffee a couple of hours ago, but it was time to either go to sleep or start the day over with strong brew.

The forgotten letter in my left hand crumpled at my side.

I'd spent all night combing the area looking for Mackenzie only to find her sitting here in the library.

But then she had disappeared right in front of my eyes. I'd turned my back for an instant and she had vanished.

How was that possible?

I picked up the letter that both Aunt Eloise and Uncle Samuel insisted that I read.

Dear Jonathan,

There's something you need to know.

I'm not the only one who travels through time.

As you know, the spell is in my blood and in the blood of our children.

I don't know if you will ever read this letter, but if you do, you have to be prepared.

Our grandchildren, Sophia, Cameron, Mackenzie, and Victoria all travel back in time from the twenty-first century to the early 1800s.

They make their lives here. What to you is the past.

THE WORDS BLURRED AND I DIDN'T READ THE REST OF THE letter. I couldn't.

I sat there. Stunned.

They were right. Aunt Eloise and Uncle Samuel. Father.

I needed to talk to my brother. Not Grant, but Nathan.

I looked at the letter again.

Sophia.

Nathan's wife was from the future.

Folding the paper and stuffing it in my pocket as I walked, I headed out to Nathan and Sophia's house.

I made the walk to their house in ten minutes. It normally took thirty.

Both of them, Nathan and Sophia, were sitting outside on a blanket watching their baby crawl from one to the other.

I knelt down at the edge of the blanket.

"Crawl to Uncle Andrew," Nathan said.

"I don't think he's here on a social visit," Sophia said, looking at me.

"I need to talk to you," I said, absently picking up the baby. I didn't know if I was talking to Nathan or Sophia. Hell, I might be talking to the baby for all I knew.

"What happened?" Nathan asked. "You look like the devil."

"I feel like the devil," I said. "Guess you managed to miss out."

"Miss out on what?" Sophia asked.

"We spent the whole night searching for her." I looked at Sophia. Knew that what I was going to say was going to rock her world. But there was no right way to say it.

"For who?" she asked, holding out her arms for the baby.

"For Mackenzie."

As I put the baby in her hands, I watched the disbelief cross her features. She held her baby against her like a shield.

"Sit," Nathan said.

I sat on the blanket and pulled the letter from my pocket. Handed it to Sophia.

41

MACKENZIE

I made it as far as the end of the driveway.

With the car blinker rhythmically ticking, I put the car in park and got out, leaving the door open.

I looked down the oak tree alley toward Grandpa's house.

Destiny.

Grandpa said it was destiny.

So I packed up my bags, loaded my car, and said my goodbyes to Grandpa.

Destiny meant I had no say in the matter.

I'd made my own way my whole life.

I'd chosen my career. Made my way to where I am by making my own choices.

Having choices made for me—already decided—was not something I was willing to sit by and let happen.

I believed in free will. That people could change. And all that.

It was what I taught. Students and clients alike.

You always have a choice.

But destiny meant there were no free choices.

If I was going to fall in love and go back in time, then I wanted it to be my own choice.

Not predetermined.

The wind of a storm coming in tossed my hair, across my face.

I shoved it back and put a hand over my eyes.

Time.

What was it?

My sister Sophia and my brother Cameron had gone back to the 1800s. It slid off the tongue as easy as saying Sophia and Cameron went to New Orleans.

As though it was as normal as simply taking a trip.

I paced to the nearest oak tree. Placed a hand against the rough bark.

Was it?

Was it as simple as taking a trip?

How was it that my parents' four children had been born in the wrong century? That they would all go back in time and marry four siblings?

Was that a thing? Four siblings marrying four siblings?

I pulled out my phone to look it up. A habit.

But I set my phone aside with a sigh. I didn't really need to know.

That wasn't the point.

The point was that Grandpa believed it had happened.

And everything I'd seen pointed in that direction.

It was quite possible that I had been back in time.

I had not seen Cameron or Sophia.

But I had met Andrew Laurent.

And my name had been written right there next to his.

There could have been another Mackenzie Becquerel.

But my name and Andrew's name were right there in a list with my siblings.

The chances of that happening too astronomical to compute. If my mother had been a history buff, then maybe she could have looked up names in the family tree to use for her own children.

But the thought of my mother doing such a thing made me laugh.

She had no interest in history or being out in the country. That was why we so rarely visited Grandpa and Grandma.

She'd cheated us on that one.

A pickup truck passing by on the road in front of me slowed, the driver rolling down his window.

"Need some help?" he asked.

"I'm good. Thank you though." I waved him off.

"I can call someone," he said.

I held up my cell phone.

He nodded and took off.

I couldn't just stand here next to the road. I got back in the car and closed the door.

The air conditioning blew in my face as the blinker continued to blink.

I pictured the day I had before me.

Drive three hours. Board a plane. Fly three hours.

Get up tomorrow and go back to my jobs.

Helping people. Teaching people.

But after forcing myself to go through that mental map of what amounted to my life, I kept seeing Andrew.

The way he looked at me.

I'd never had a man look at me that way.

The first night had been a night of passion. Gentlemanly passion.

The next time we'd been together had been different.

He'd been courting me.

And wanted to ask my brother for permission to court me.

I knew what courting meant. It was an old-fashioned way of saying dating.

But I looked it up. So help me, I unlocked my phone and looked it up.

To engage in social activities leading to engagement and marriage.

I leaned back against the car seat, squeezing the steering wheel.

Damn it.

Andrew wanted to *marry* me.

The strong handsome man from the 1850s who had stolen my heart wanted to marry me.

And Grandpa believed it was destiny.

I could drive away from here.

Go back to work.

Help other people.

But who was going to help me?

Who was going to help me get through day after day of thinking about Andrew? About the way his lips felt on mine. The way his body felt against mine.

The way I'd come against him and he'd asked for nothing in return.

He'd spent his whole night looking for me. When I'd been right there in the library… sleeping in the chair.

As I sat watching dark clouds coming in from the southwest, I realized something.

Something so counterintuitive that it made me laugh at myself.

I had a choice.

In this moment. I have a choice.

42

ANDREW

I spent the rest of the day with Nathan and Sophia.

They were so obviously in love, it was almost hard to watch at times, especially knowing that I had come so very close to having something similar with Mackenzie.

Sophia had not said much about the letter.

I think it caught her so very off guard that she did not have much to say about it.

She'd taken her baby inside and, although I could not see what she was doing, I would bet money that she was taking time to digest it all.

When she came back outside a bit later, her eyes were red.

Nathan took the baby and handed her to me, then pulled his wife into his arms.

"Are you okay?" he asked.

She shrugged and attempted a smile.

"Not really," I heard her tell Nathan.

"I need to talk to Andrew."

So I handed the baby to Nathan and went for a walk with my sister-in-law.

We walked along the river, the mournful sound of a paddle wheeler filling the air.

"You've spent some time with Mackenzie?" she asked, lifting the hem of her skirt to avoid a mud puddle as we walked past.

"Yes," I said. "A little."

She looked at me sideways.

"A little?"

"Enough," I said with a little smile.

"You want to court her?" she asked.

"You know I do."

She nodded. "That's why you showed me that letter."

She already knew the answer to that.

The paddle wheeler disappeared over the horizon leaving the river empty. A rare sight on the busy Mississippi.

"You don't know her," she said.

I could tell by the way she said it that she knew she'd just made an irrelevant observation.

"I know what I need to know," I said.

"Right." Looking away, she nodded. I couldn't read her expression. But I knew I needed to tread carefully. I was talking about her sister. I could hardly tell her that I had been in her bed... or rather, technically, she had been in my bed.

Either way. My intentions were honorable if she would have me, I would marry her.

Turning toward me, she put a hand on my arm. Searched my eyes.

"Andrew," she said. "your reputation..." She cleared her throat. "I'll just ask it straight out. What are your intentions toward my sister?"

"You can rest assured." I smiled slowly. I could see the resemblance to Mackenzie in Sophia's eyes. "My intentions toward your sister are entirely honorable. If she'll have me..."

Sophia turned and started walking again.

"I know my sister," she said. "Mackenzie doesn't believe in fate. But…" She stopped again and gazed across the river.

The blood pounded in my ears. If Mackenzie did not believe in fate… then what did that mean?

"If she comes back to you… if she finds a way." Mackenzie paused. "Then she's yours."

"Is there anything I can do?"

"Maybe," she said. "How certain are you? About her?"

"I've never been more certain about anything."

"Okay." Sophia said. "You can get a message to her."

43

MACKENZIE

Grandpa sat at the kitchen table. His newspaper carefully folded and set aside.

I paced the kitchen. Stopped and leaned against the sink to look outside.

He had not looked surprised to see me.

On the contrary. He's simply opened the door and I'd followed him back to the kitchen.

Wind whipped at the silvery gray moss. This place was a like a vortex for storms.

Coalescing right here. A rip in time, according to the legend. A rip in time would attract storm, I suppose.

Turning, I faced Grandpa.

How could he look so calm? Maybe he was like me. Even when there was a storm on the inside, I kept my expression impassive. In fact, the more emotion I felt, the more I kept it to myself.

A psychologist must remain in control at all times.

We were the lifeline for others. The lifeboat. If the lifeboat sank, everyone sank.

It was who I was. I could not change that.

But on the inside I was as human as the rest.

"Besides the notes in the Bible?" I asked. "Is there any other way to know? To know how Andrew feels? Now that he's met me."

Grandpa sat back. Ran a hand across his balding head.

I wondered how much stress all this had put his through. So many people he had loved had gone back in time.

Everyone in fact that he loved. Lost to time.

How did he do it?

Had he ever wished to go back in time?

"Maybe," Grandpa said, pushing back in his chair. "There is one other place to look."

I followed him down the hall, through the foyer past the silent grandfather clock, up the stairs. To the guest room.

He grabbed a pry bar from the closet and went to kneel in front of the window. The casing on the left was different. Newer wood. The other three sides were old, weathered, probably original wood.

"What are we doing?" I asked.

He turned and grinned at me as he slid the pry bar beneath the newer casing.

"We're checking the mail," he said.

The mail.

I sat back on my heels and watched as a rolled-up letter fell out as he loosened the casing.

"We've got mail," he said, picking up the letter and sitting back on a little stool.

A letter.

He carefully unrolled the letter. Glanced at it.

"It's from your sister," he said. "It's for you."

My hands shook as I took the letter he held out to me.

"I don't understand," I said, searching his eyes.

"Sophia and I worked this out a long time ago," he said. "She writes letters and puts them here. In the past. And since this is… was… an original window casing, I can find them here in our time."

I ran a hand along the paper. It didn't feel old.

"It's alkaline paper," he said. "She took it with her. It's supposed to last hundreds of years."

I swallowed, my throat dry and tried to focus on the words.

Dear Grandpa and Mackenzie,

I looked up at Grandpa. "How did she know?"

"She's been at this for a long time." He shrugged.

I kept reading.

I have a letter here for Mackenzie from Andrew.

Love you both,

Sophia

Dear Mackenzie,

Not sure how... or if... this works, but if it does, then I figure you're trying to make a choice.

I fell in love with you the moment I saw you. At the piano. You play the piano like an angel.

If you're trying to decide what to do, then I hope this letter helps.

The decision is yours.

But I will wait for you. Forever.

Just know that.

I'm here. Waiting for you.

I love you.

Please come back to me.

Andrew

. . .

My eyes moist, I turned and looked at Grandpa. Handed the letter to him.

It didn't matter that it was written to me. This wasn't something I could process alone.

Grandpa read the letter, then handed it back to me.

"The ball's in your court, Kitten," he said.

44

ANDREW

Sophia tapped the window casing back into place and sat back on her heels.

"What now?" I asked.

She shrugged. "We wait."

We wait.

I'd said I'd wait forever.

Forever was a long time.

I got up and went to the window.

So, the way I understood it… we wrote a letter on some kind of special paper that was supposed to last centuries. Hid it behind the window casing.

Then Sophia and Mackenzie's Grandpa would look behind this very same window casing centuries later. And it would still be there.

It was incomprehensible.

And fascinating.

She assured me that it could work. She'd written her brother, Cameron, and he had gotten the letter.

"How long?" I asked, unable to help myself.

She smiled.

"On our end it could be a minute or twenty years."

I turned back to look out the window.

The old oak trees planted a hundred years ago by the Frenchman who had claimed this land for himself stood tall and strong.

Did they still stand hundreds of years in the future? It was something I had never even thought about until this moment.

If this house still stood, then surely the trees did. They would be bigger, of course.

"Andrew," Sophia said, interrupting my musings. "Time isn't linear like you'd think. It could be ten years for her and overnight for us."

"Okay." I did not understand any of what she was telling me.

"I'm saying you have to be prepared."

"Prepared for what?"

"It's possible she could be older."

"I don't care," I said, realizing that I actually did not care.

I'd fallen head over heels for Mackenzie. It was a new and wonderful experience.

"Please bring her to see me when she gets here, okay?" Sophia said.

"Of course." I held out a hand to help her up. "You should get back to Nathan and your baby."

She would come back.

She had to.

In the meantime, I would not be sitting idle.

I had things I had to do.

First I needed to talk to Father and Uncle Samuel about some land.

Now that I had my patch of tobacco growing, it was time to break ground on a house.

Mine and Mackenzie's.

45

MACKENZIE

"Our time is up, Paul," I said, closing my notepad and setting it aside.

The last of the evening sunshine cast shadows through the west facing window opened to catch the soft fall breeze.

My chairs were positioned so that I could see the peaks of the Rocky Mountains from here. It was by design. What could I say? My days were long and sometimes I just needed to rest my eyes.

"I know," he said. "Are you sure I'm ready to go it on my own?"

Paul had been one of my first clients. I was about as reluctant to let him go as he was to let me go. But it was time.

He had a good job. A fiancé. His scores on the Depression Inventory had been consistently low over the past six months.

His eyes were moist, but it wasn't from depression. It was because it was time to say goodbye.

I felt the same way.

A professional relationship was still at its heart a relationship. Paul had been a good client. He'd spilled his deepest darkest secrets to me and he'd been willing to try anything I threw at him.

And as an experienced psychologist, I'm sure that had been interesting at times.

"You're going to be just fine," I said.

"Can I have a hug?" he asked, tentatively.

"Of course." Breaking one of my own rules as I gave him a quick hug.

"Now go," I said. "Have a good life."

That got a laugh out of Paul and he headed out.

I sat down at my little computer desk and blew out a breath.

Picked up a bottle of water while the program loaded up.

I typed in Paul's confidential notes, then entered the insurance information and submitted that.

Done. A chapter closed.

Cleared out for the next one.

I unlocked my phone and ordered from my favorite to go restaurant. I'd pick it up on the way home.

Do some reading while I ate.

Then I needed to call my sister, Victoria.

I had a lot to tell her.

A LOT to tell her.

I had a couple of other calls to make, too, but I could do those on the drive home.

I stuffed my computer in my computer bag along with my charging cords.

Pushed the chair up to the desk and plumped the back pillow on the armchair where I had spent countless hours listening to people tell me their innermost thoughts.

Helped them make difficult life choices and work through troubles.

I'd learned a lot about myself by helping them.

To be perfectly honest, I'd probably learned more about myself than my clients had learned about themselves.

But that was the way of it. Teachers learned more than students. Psychologists learned more than clients.

Squaring my shoulders, I stepped out of the office, locked the door, and slipped the key in my bag.

We have to do something different if we want things to change.

It was time for a change.

46

ANDREW

Balancing on top of the roof—my roof—I hammered nails into another of the wood shingles.

The sun was warm on the top of my head in contrast to the coolness of the breeze coming off the river.

I'd taken my time on the house. Father and Grant had helped some. Even Uncle Samuel had hammered a few nails.

But today I was alone. But whether alone or not, I enjoyed the process. I was building something special for someone special.

It had been a year and some months since I'd seen Mackenzie, but I thought about her every day. She was the first thing I thought about when I woke in the morning. The last thing I thought about when I went to sleep at night.

As the days flew past, I did not give up. She was worth waiting for.

I'd wait my whole life if I had to.

A steamboat floated past, blowing its mournful whistle. I couldn't imagine the river without the steamboat horns.

The sun was starting its nightly dip behind the trees. It was quitting time.

Time for me to gather up my tools for the night and go to the main house for a drink and probably some entertainment if things went as expected.

I couldn't say that Emma had gotten any better at playing the piano, but I could say that I had perhaps lowered my expectations such that I could tolerate her music a bit better.

I'd taken to leaning against the wall, closing my eyes, and using the quiet time to think about Mackenzie. It was time when no one expected me to have a conversation.

A time when no one hinted that I should consider courting one of the *fine young ladies in the area.*

And so, in an odd way, I'd rather come to appreciate Emma's piano music.

After tossing my tools down, I climbed down the ladder.

There were dark clouds coming in tonight. But I didn't hear any thunder, so it was probably just going to be one of those ever so calm soaking rains that lasted for days.

It was odd, really, how I had come to prefer stormy nights.

During any thunderstorm, I could be found sitting on the steps overlooking the foyer in the main house.

Listening to the grandfather clock as it tolled the hour, the lightning crashing all around us.

I watched every movement. Every shadow.

One day Mackenzie would come back to me.

I believed it with every cell in my body.

I lived it. Breathed it.

As I headed back to the house, Charlie and her three puppies raced up to escort me home.

Soon, I mused, with puppies tumbling over each other at my feet, this would be home.

I didn't like the idea of living here alone without the woman I was building it for, but it was time to get out of my uncle's house.

Father as dragging his feet on his own house. I think that as the adult children left home, getting places of their own, he was questioning building a house just for him and Mother.

Nobody knew what Grant was going to do. He held his cards close to his chest. I halfway expected him to up and announce one day that he was going back to New Orleans.

I went in through the back door, poured myself a glass of whiskey, and headed upstairs to get cleaned up for the evening.

47

MACKENZIE

I leaned against the balcony railing looking out over the gardens below.

Grandpa had enlisted Tracie's help to get the flower garden back in shape. Of course, now that it was Fall, they would have to plants some fall flowers.

The scent of daffodils, roses, and magnolias filled the air.

Tracie was here all the time now. They'd negotiated room and board as part of her pay.

After I got past the guilt of not having the time to give to be here for him myself, I was pleased that he had Tracie.

She seemed to be good for him. And had turned out to be trustworthy.

She had a lot of good qualities that were hard to find.

I'd set up my financials so that Grandpa would get everything I had. Between his and mine, he would never be short on money.

I had three weather apps on my phone. There were others, but I didn't see any reason to over do it.

Since it was the trailing end of hurricane season, there was no way to predict when the next storm would hit.

But I was ready.

For now, the weather was quiet. Clear and beautiful.

I was wearing my favorite pajama bottoms—the ones with the teddy bears on them and a plain gray t-shirt.

Feeling restless, I grabbed a sweatshirt, tossed it over my head, and headed downstairs.

Grandpa and Tracie were playing cards at the kitchen table.

"Want to pull up a chair?" Grandpa asked.

"No, No." I said, grabbing a bottle of water. "Don't let me disturb you."

They assured me I was welcome, but I was too restless to sit and play a game.

I made my way toward the foyer, stopping to look up at the grandfather clock. The key was there, just inside the glass door.

The key that held the secret to the time travel.

Sometimes it worked. Sometimes it wasn't necessary for the time travel to happen.

It was not an exact science.

Sort of like psychology, I mused.

There were theories and things that worked sometimes, but not always. Depended on the situation.

Yep. Just like psychology.

I wandered into the parlor and paced to the window. The night was clear. The moon bright.

Feeling disappointed, I went to the piano and sat down. Rested my fingers on the keys.

I didn't want to disturb anyone, but Grandpa and Tracie were playing cards.

There was no reason not to play.

I pressed one key. Let the note hold in the air. Then I pressed another one. And they blended together.

My fingers took off then on the keys, almost as though of their own accord.

I always wondered if maybe I should have pursued music instead of psychology.

The melancholy music that poured out through my fingers had me thinking about regrets.

I did not want to have any more regrets.

It had not taken me long after returning to Denver to know that I did not want to play out my life there, doing the same thing day after day, over and over.

It wasn't me anymore.

My heart belonged to someone in the past.

And without sharing a heart, what purpose was there, really?

It was like music.

I could go the safe route and choose to stay here in my safe time.

Closing my eyes, I let the music spill over me, letting it blur my thoughts, taking the edge off my nerves.

It was nice to just stop thinking for a minute.

To just let my mind go blank.

48

ANDREW

I was lured back downstairs by the music.

Not Emma's music.

The melancholy music that I knew could only come from Mackenzie.

As I went down the stairs, I kept my hands in my pockets to keep them from shaking.

She was here then.

Or was it like before when either I was there or we were nowhere?

I'd had a lot of time to think. And I'd spent a lot of time talking to Sophia and Nathan.

I would have talked to my sister's husband, Cameron, but they lived in town and he spent all his time working. Writing books.

It was actually impressive how well he was doing.

But right now, after all this time, she was here.

My feet touched the first floor and I walked slowly past the grandfather clock.

The music faltered when the clock began to chime. It was just for a moment, but I heard that.

That told me that Mackenzie heard it, too.

But she kept playing.

Mon Dieu. She had an unparalleled way with the piano.

Reaching the door to the parlor, I stopped and just watched her.

Sophia had warned me that Mackenzie might be older now, but she was as young and beautiful as she had been before.

I slowly moved around so that I was standing in front of her.

She played with her eyes closed.

Obviously she had no need to see the notes on the sheet music.

How was it that she could play like this out of her head?

Sophia hadn't said anything to me about Mackenzie being a pianist. She'd told me that Mackenzie was a physician of the mind.

I did not understand that, but anything was possible in the future.

I looked forward to learning more about Mackenzie and the world where she had come from.

Finally, as the rain splashed against the windows, her music slowed and she sat with her fingers resting on the keys.

A tremor of concern chased down my spine when she did not open her eyes.

She sat very still like a statue.

I took a step forward.

Then she opened her eyes and looked at me.

"Are you real?" she asked, so softly I could barely hear her.

"Yes," I said.

Then she was up, off the bench, and in my arms.

I had my arms full of Mackenzie Becquerel.

"How do I keep you here?" I asked, cupping her face with my hands.

She shook her head and kissed me.

Then she pulled back to gaze into my eyes.

"Faith," she said. "We have to have faith."

"I have faith," I said. "I built you a house."

"A house?" She searched my eyes for answers. "How?"

"Your sister drew the plans."

Mackenzie took a step back, her hands over her mouth.

"Sophia?"

"Yes." I grinned. "She made me promise to bring you by her home."

"Oh," Mackenzie said. "She really has a home."

I put my arms around her waist and twirled her around. She laughed.

"You will marry me, right?" I asked, setting her on her feet and kissing her cheeks.

"Well," she shrugged. "I did come all this way. So…."

I took a deep breath and forced myself to take a step back.

I was going to marry this woman. I had just one time to get it right.

This was not the time to rush.

But I just wanted to be with her. To have her bound to me so that not even time could pull us apart again.

49

MACKENZIE

I'd known Andrew was there before I even opened my eyes.

Maybe it was the rain pounding against the windows. Rain on a perfectly clear night with not a drop of rain in the forecast.

He was so beautiful. So handsome.

Maybe even more than I remembered.

He wanted me to marry him.

And I wanted to marry him.

I really had come all this way.

He took a step back and went down on one knee.

Holding both my hands, he looked up into my eyes.

"Mackenzie," he said. "Since I couldn't ask your father or your grandfather for your hand, I asked your sister."

Sophia… I was having a little trouble following what he was saying.

I never had trouble following people. It was what I did for a living.

The blood rushing through my veins, pounding through my system, had me off balance.

"Mackenzie," he said. "Will you do me the honor of being my wife?"

"Yes," I said, barely able to get the word out.

To say that I was overcome with emotion was an understatement.

I couldn't catch my breath.

Then Andrew put his hands on either side of my face and kissed me ever so lightly.

His lips against mine centered me.

Brought me back to my senses and I could breathe again.

"You built us a house?" I asked, against his lips.

"Yes… Well… I'm building a house. It's not finished."

"When can I see it?"

"Tomorrow," he said. "weather permitting."

"I can't wait to see it."

"It's not far," he said. "And it's close to Sophia's."

"Wait…" I said. I wanted to ask, but I was afraid of the answer. "My brother… Cameron?"

"He lives in town with his wife, Isabella." Andrew smiled.

I let out a sigh of relief. "He's okay, then?"

"He is more than okay. He is happily married. To my sister."

"Right. Your sister."

It seemed so wrong yet so right at the same time. Brothers and sisters marrying brothers and sisters.

Somehow me and my siblings had been born in the wrong century.

There was our other sister, Victoria, but I'd worry about her later.

Right now all I wanted to do was to kiss Andrew.

Apparently, he had the same idea. He reached down and picking me up, carried me to the bottom of the stairs.

"You have to put me down now," I said.

"I can carry you up the stairs," he said, but let me slide to my feet.

"Only if you're Clark Gable," I said, kissing him on the jaw.

"I don't know who that is, but it sounds like we have a lot to talk about."

"More than you can imagine," I said.

We walked upstairs, hand in hand.

Then he picked me up again and carried to the door of his… my… our… room.

But this time, he didn't set me down. This time he carried me over the threshold and laid me on the bed.

The steady rain came down outside, splashing against the window, enveloping us in a safe, dry cocoon.

It was real. It was so unbelievably real.

I felt like I'd been working my whole life to get right here. To this moment.

To this this place and this time.

Destiny.

It wasn't such a bad thing after all.

50

MACKENZIE

Two weeks later

We married quickly. Not because we had to, but because we wanted to.

Andrew and I both agreed that marriage may well be the thing that not only bound us together, but the thing that locked me into this time.

We weren't willing to rule anything out.

The Becquerel house was overflowing with people. Inside and outside. It was one of those lovely fall evenings when the weather was perfect.

And tonight I did not mind the perfect weather.

The Becquerels had invited everyone to the reception following our small family-only wedding ceremony.

But the six of us had slipped off into the library after just one dance. Considering that three of us were desperately unskilled at waltzing, it made perfect sense.

I don't know why we closed the inside door. The French doors were open letting lively orchestra music spill inside.

Guests were waltzing… drinking punch—spiked… and gossip abounded.

I sat on the little sofa next to Andrew, my wedding dress spilling over his lap with enough material to make twenty regular dresses. He had one arm around me and toyed with his top hat he had borrowed from Cameron with the other. There was something significant about that, but I didn't question it. I'd find out later.

My sister Sophia sat in an armchair across from us. Nathan stood behind her leaning against the chair. An old married couple now with a child.

Our brother Cameron sat on the other armchair, his wife Isabella, in his lap. Happily married for over a year, but still acting like newlyweds. Isabella's reputation for being serious had evaporated under my brother's influence.

"It's so strange how we all ended up together," Sophia said. "in the same place and time, but in a different century from where we started."

"Don't think about it too hard," Cameron said. "It'll make your head hurt."

"What do you think, Mackenzie?" Sophia asked, and everyone looked at me.

"I'm just listening," I said.

"Oh no," Cameron said. "You don't get to pull that psychologist stuff on us."

"Well," I said, looking into Andrew's eyes. "I thought I was having hallucinations."

Sophia and Cameron laughed. They understood.

"She kept asking me if I was real," Andrew said, pulling me against him.

"I sort of stopped caring," I said with a little shrug.

Andrew kissed me on the cheek. "You'd rather be with me than in reality."

"Yes," I said, kissing him on the lips.

"Don't you all have another sister?" Nathan asked, distracting us.

Everyone knew we did.

"Victoria," Sophia said.

"Do you think Victoria will be coming?" Andrew asked. He asked it as though she would just be stopping by.

"Victoria will not set foot on this property." Cameron scoffed. "So no. It's not possible."

"It's on the paper," I said, softly.

Cameron shook his head. "She won't do it."

"Why won't she come here?" Nathan asked as he went over to the liquor cabinet. Put six glasses and a bottle of champagne on a tray.

His question was met with silence.

"Nobody wants to talk about that," Sophia said as he put the tray on the coffee table and sat down on the arm of the chair.

"Another family secret," he said as he filled the first glass with champagne. Handed it to me.

Then handed another to Andrew.

I grinned at Andrew over the bubbles.

"Don't drink too much," he whispered for my ears only. "I have plans for you tonight."

I laughed.

"Hey," Cameron said. "Get a room."

Andrew and I looked at each other and shrugged.

"To happy time travel and forever marriages," he said, raising a glass.

We all raised our glasses in a toast.

Except for Sophia. Sophia slowly set her glass down.

"Sophia?"

She looked at Nathan and grinned.

"We're having a baby." Nathan pulled her close and kissed her on the mouth.

Right about then, the door opened and Uncle Samuel stuck his head inside. We all sat quietly, holding our glasses.

"There you are," he said. "Everyone is looking for the newlyweds."

"Might as well go," Nathan said. "Or there will be no hearing the end of it."

"That's God's honest truth," Andrew said, standing up and pulling me to my feet.

Three couples, the women all dressed in bright colorful dresses, on the arms of their handsome formally dressed men, spilled out of the library and headed toward the foyer.

The grandfather clock began tolling the hour, the loud chimes mingling in with the music.

Andrew pulled my hand, making sure we hung back as the others went into the foyer.

"Come on," he said, tugging my hand and pulling me toward the stairs.

"What?" I asked.

"Let's get out of here," he said.

"But the reception is—"

He shot me a look.

"Do you want to hang out with strangers or do you want get started on your wedding night?"

"Well…" I said. "When you put it like that."

Our hands tightly linked, he led us straight up the stairs.

We reached the second floor just as the clock chimed the twelfth hour.

Midnight.

This time Cinderella was running away from the ball WITH the prince.

And there would be no turning into a pumpkin.

This time it was for real.

Keep Reading for a Preview of Promised in the Mist…

PROMISED IN THE MIST PREVIEW

Prologue

It was a given that a fifteen-year-old boy left to his own devices in the country would get into trouble.

Grant Laurent was no exception.

Today it was hot as the devil, so he had done what any reasonable teen would do. He had gone down to the murky, smelly Mississippi River bank to hunt frogs.

He'd been successful, too. He had a big son-of-a-bitching bull frog in his burlap bag. It kicked and squeaked, but he'd let it out soon enough. He wasn't cruel. He had good plans for it, though, before he set it free.

Hell, his cousins would probably want to eat it. Northerners —and yes, Natchez was the north compared to New Orleans— were strange people.

Walking along the road leading away from the river toward the house, he slung the sack over his shoulder and whistled a nonsensible tune.

He was the only one outside. Everyone else was inside, avoiding the hottest part of the sunny day. But not Grant. Grant was a man with a purpose. And today's purpose was to send his sister squealing.

A flock of blue birds fluttered from one of the old oak trees, taking flight into the cloudless sky.

That was definitely one of the benefits—few as they were—to spending summers up here in the country. There was far more to get into.

His parents packed up the whole family and traveled here every year for the three or four hottest months of the summer.

Mother was deathly afraid of contracting the yellow fever. Father's parents had both died from it before Grant was even born, but it left a lasting impression on Mother.

Following the bend in the road, he could see the house up ahead. A huge three-story house with tall white columns from ground to roof. He personally preferred his town home in New Orleans with the courtyard right in the middle, but this was the style out here in the country.

A cool breeze swept through the trees, sending the moss flying like silver flags on a pirate ship.

He shivered. This was full on June. There should be no cool spells. Maybe a little cool in the mornings, but that burned off quick enough.

There were some dark clouds banking in the southwest. If they were in New Orleans, he'd say there was a hurricane coming in. But they were much too far inland for that.

He shrugged it off and kept walking.

It made no difference to him. He had his frog and he was happy.

As he rounded another bend, he noticed that there was a layer of mist coming in. The kind of mist that sometimes lingering over the Mississippi River early in the mornings.

Now that was weird.

He stopped and looked behind him, but the mist was everywhere. And he was alone.

He took another step, but something invisible seemed to push back, keeping him from going any further.

He would expected something like this in New Orleans, but it was the first time he'd encountered anything other than the mundane up here.

Intrigued, but like most fifteen-year-old boys, not afraid of anything, he turned around again to see what he could see behind him.

He couldn't see anything other than the mist, but it what he didn't see… didn't hear… that was most interesting.

He didn't hear anything at all. No steamboat whistle. No dogs braying at squirrels. No birds.

He slowly turned back around, ready to get on to the house now.

Enough was enough already.

His feet froze to the ground, this time of their own accord.

A girl, about his age, stood not more than three feet in front of him.

The wind whipped at her long black hair. She stood perfectly still, not bothering to sweep it out of her eyes.

She was wearing nothing but a pair of short blue pants that left her legs scandalously bear all the way down to a pair of white shoes. Her top was equally risqué. A tight light blue material that left her arms bare. The scooped neck accented her bosom.

He took in all of this with a split-second glance, but it was her eyes that enchanted him.

Big green eyes framed with thick dark lashes. Her skin was white as snow and her lips red and plush.

She was frowning at him from that beautiful face.

He just grinned in response. Confronted with such beauty

looking at him with adorable consternation, there was nothing else he could do.

The mist swirled at their feet, but they were alone in a cocoon of silence.

Then the wind stopped blowing her hair. It just stopped.

The moss in the trees around us still blew in the wind, but within their little bubble, there was no sound. No wind. Nothing but mist swirling at their feet.

They tried again to take a step forward. Managed one step.

He swallowed the emotion that overwhelmed him and took another step forward.

If she was really there, he wanted to touch her. To feel her.

She, too, took a step forward and now he were standing merely inches apart.

She looked up at me with her beautiful green eyes, framed with long thick lashes, her mouth parted ever so slightly. Her breathing was shallow as though she had just run a long distance. And he felt much the same way.

"I can't…" He held up a hand, palm out, unable to get his thoughts formed into words. "Are you real?"

She held her own hand up, her palm facing, but not touching, his.

"I'm real," she said.

They stood there with our hands held up as though they stood on two sides of a window, able to see each other, but unable to actually touch.

But it wasn't enough. Would never be enough.

He wanted to actually touch her.

To know that she was real.

"As am I," he said, searching her eyes.

Then unable to stop himself, he pressed his hand forward, clasping her fingers in his.

She was real. She was so very real.

Now that he had touched her, he couldn't get enough.

He lifted his other hand, with every intent of taking her other hand, too, but that did not happen.

She began to fade.

Her fingers slipped out of his. He leaned forward, trying to keep his grip on her.

But the girl quite simply faded away.

The mist receded along with the wind and the cool breeze. A steamboat blew its familiar horn on the river behind him and a dog brayed.

His burlap sack had fallen to the ground and the frog escaped.

But he no longer cared.

All he cared about was the girl who had just vanished in front of his eyes.

Chapter 1

Victoria Becquerel

I WAS ONLY HERE TO GET THE CAT.

And take care of a few of Grandpa Jonathan's financials.

The house was clean, but it just smelled… well… old. Musty really.

I was used to the antiseptic scent of the hospital where I worked. So much so that anything else smelled dirty.

The furry white cat jumped on top of the breakfast table as I pulled the lid on a can of cat food and set it there in front of him. I didn't care if he ate on the table.

But he just sat there and blinked at me.

"What?" I asked.

The cat meowed.

"Oh. Alright." It took me a minute to find a saucer to dump

the cat food into it. I slid it over. The cat dove in, like he hadn't eaten in days.

Kit Kat. That was his name. Kit Kat sounded like a girl's name to me, but who was I to judge.

As the cat lapped up his food, I put my hands on my hips and looked around the kitchen, trying to decide what else needed to be done.

I had vowed to never set foot here again.

But my siblings were unreachable.

My sister, Sophia, had disappeared eleven years ago, never to be found.

Just another reason for me to hate this place.

And now my other two siblings, Cameron and Mackenzie, wouldn't answer their phones. Straight to voice mail. Both of them.

What if it was important?

It was important.

Grandpa would be spending a month in rehab.

His assistant… caregiver… Tracie… had called me in tears.

Grandpa had left specific instructions that I was the one to be called in case of emergency.

Maybe because I was a doctor. Maybe because the other ones couldn't be reached and Grandpa knew it.

I'd asked Tracie to take the cat, but she said no. And no, she didn't know anyone else who could take care of him.

That's what happened when a person lived thirty minutes out of town.

You had no friends. And if you did have friends, they weren't going to spend half a day driving out to feed a cat everyday.

For an entire month.

Out of options, I'd driven here from Atlanta just to get the cat.

Just because I didn't want to be here was no reason for the cat to starve while Grandpa was in rehab.

I needed to try to see Grandpa, but what I really needed to do was to get back to Atlanta.

So I had a couple of other things to do, then I was going to throw the cat in his carrier and head out of here.

I had my reasons for not wanting to be here at the Becquerel estate. It had nothing to do with my family. Nothing to do with Grandpa.

And it had everything to do with an experience I'd had when I was just fifteen years old.

An experience I'd had in the mist.

I'd never told a single soul.

But I'd never forgotten it.

And never would.

Chapter 2

Grant Laurent

THE SOIL UP HERE IN THE NORTHERN PART OF THE STATE WAS good. I couldn't complain about that.

The little cotton plants were just now starting to peek up through the soil. Seeing that was my favorite part of the whole planting process. To me it was magical how the little seeds knew how to find their way out of the dirt so they could start growing into big productive plants.

Also, here in mid-March, the weather was still bearable. Pleasant even. I removed my hat to run a hand through my hair, the warm sun beating down on my head.

My horse, Fair Flax, shifted beneath me crinkling the leather of my saddle.

He shook his head at the mournful wail of a steamboat's horn as it passed. He'd heard the sound his entire life. Even down south. Maybe it was his way of greeting the boat.

I waved.

Didn't know if they could see me or not, but I waved anyway. It was the neighborly thing to do.

Somehow I'd gotten the reputation of being standoffish.

I couldn't figure out what was wrong about a man wanting to keep his head down and doing his work.

I didn't gamble or drink much or visit Natchez Under the Hill.

And I didn't dance with every marriageable girl in the county.

In fact, when I did attend a ball or picnic out of family obligation, I rarely danced at all.

Contrary to common belief, not every eligible bachelor was in need of a wife.

Now. What I could complain about was only having two acres for my cotton fields.

How exactly was a man supposed to make a success of himself with only two measly acres?

But since I did not want to be an ingrate, I kept my mouth shut about it and had been asking around to see if there was some nearby land I could purchase.

Waiting around to see what my father was going to do as far as dividing up his property between himself and his three sons was one thing. But I was not getting any younger.

The other thing I could complain about was being up here in north Mississippi to begin with.

Our plantation home outside of New Orleans had burned to the ground. Father's property to be technical. So he'd sold the land and the townhome to pay some debts.

There was supposed to be enough money left over to build a house on my mother's dowry land up here.

But Father, it seemed, at least to me, had all but decided to just live with Uncle Samuel and his wife.

Made since though, because my brother Nathan had built a home of his own for his wife and family. My other brother Andrew was doing the same. In the meantime, they lived here in the main house, but that wouldn't last for long.

My sister had a husband to take care of her and they lived in town.

That just left me.

I was accustomed to managing thousands of acres. Now I was down to two. Two acres.

Next year was going to be different.

I would figure something out.

I had not always been the serious one, I mused, as I turned Fair Flax around to head for home.

I'd actually been the mischievous one until that day long ago.

That had been the last summer I'd spent here until now.

That was the summer I'd seen the girl in the mist.

It had changed the way I saw the world.

It had changed everything about me.

And I had never told a living soul.

Keep Reading Promised in the Mist…

Kathryn Kaleigh is the author of sixty-eight novels, over one hundred short stories, and many collections.

kathrynkaleigh.com

www.ingramcontent.com/pod-product-compliance
Lightning Source LLC
Chambersburg PA
CBHW030337310726
48979CB00001B/74

* 9 7 8 1 6 4 7 9 1 3 9 4 6 *